ALL MY WITCHES
A WICKED WITCHES OF THE MIDWEST FANTASY

~~~

AMANDA M. LEE

WINCHESTERSHAW PUBLICATIONS

Copyright © 2018 by Amanda M. Lee

All rights reserved.

No part of this book may be reproduced in any form or by any electronic or mechanical means, including information storage and retrieval systems, without written permission from the author, except for the use of brief quotations in a book review.

❦ Created with Vellum

Soaps shouldn't handle real-life stuff like school shootings and health care reform. They should stick to the important stuff like time travel, music montages and evil twins. If I want to watch real-life stuff I'll opt for the news … which is completely boring to think about.

– Clove on what's important in regard to storytelling

ONE

"Don't make me come out there!"

I glared at the door that separated The Overlook's kitchen from the dining room, my temper flaring as I pictured what sat on the other side. Or rather, who.

I could practically see her.

She would be sitting in her recliner, a mug of coffee on the counter, her feet buried under a blanket, a plate of cookies on her lap and her eyes trained on the small television where she preferred to watch her stories when it was cold.

Most people would find it an adorable sight, a grandmotherly figure cuddling up to spend her afternoon lost in a fantasy world.

I know better.

I know her.

"Don't make me come in there!" I shot back, my temper getting the better of me.

That's right. I, Bay Winchester, am officially out of patience. Under normal circumstances, I'm the one calling off my cousin Thistle when she decides to move on Aunt Tillie. These battles are generally an attempt to make the woman come to heel, or act like a normal great-aunt. You know, stop selling pot or threatening to curse us within an inch of our lives. I was feeling something different today, although I couldn't put a name to it.

"I'll make you wish you'd never been born if you don't shut your mouth," Aunt Tillie barked. I couldn't see her but that didn't make the sound of her voice any less grating. "I already wish you hadn't been born, so we're almost there, you little witch."

My eyes flashed as I moved to push myself to a standing position, but my mother stilled me with a hand to my shoulder. Winnie Winchester was used to the endless fights. That didn't mean she liked them.

"You need to let it go." Mom was calm, her face reflecting a serenity that I couldn't possibly share. "You're making things worse."

My eyebrows flew up my forehead. "I'm making things worse?" How was that even possible? Aunt Tillie is the queen of making things worse. "She's the one who said … well, you heard what she said."

"I did," Mom confirmed. "That's hardly the worst thing she's said this week. Heck, it's not even the worst thing she's said today. Before you showed up, Aunt Tillie told Twila she was going to buy one of those ball gags used for … um, sex games … and make her wear it if she didn't stop trying to talk to her.

"Twila had no idea what she was talking about, so she looked it up on the internet," she continued. "Then she started screaming and carrying on – just like you are right now – and now we have to call a computer technician because I'm pretty sure Twila downloaded a virus from one of those sex sites."

I pressed my lips together, unsure if I wanted to join forces with Twila and call Aunt Tillie on her crap or simply burst out laughing because imagining Twila's reaction to all the porn would keep me entertained for weeks to come. Finally, I merely shrugged. "Aunt Tillie is evil."

It was a simple statement, appropriately dark and pointed. Mom didn't look bothered by my assessment.

"She is," Mom agreed. "But in this particular case, you're the one in the wrong. She's in there minding her own business … ."

I balked. "She's not minding her own business. She never minds her own business. She pretends to mind her own business while really taking an invisible needle the size of my arm and poking people with it when she thinks they're not looking. That's not minding her business."

Mom pressed the tip of her tongue to her top lip as she debated how to answer. I didn't give her a chance.

"That woman is up to no good," I added. "She's plotting the downfall of civilization. In fact ... yeah, I've given it some thought and I know this is true. I'm pretty sure she traveled through time and took down the Roman Empire. Also, there's a very good chance she's the one who crashed Amelia Earhart's plane. Oh ... and you know that thing in Roanoke? Totally her."

Mom made a derisive sound in the back of her throat. "I'm so glad your head is in a good place. I can't tell you how proud it makes me to know that you're not unbalanced ... or potentially psychotic ... or frustratingly stubborn ... at all."

I didn't care. "She's evil," I repeated.

"That's hardly news."

"Who is evil?" My cousin Thistle asked as she breezed into the room. Her hair, which was four different colors this week (she was trying something new), was covered with snow. Thistle learned to be evil at Aunt Tillie's knee, so she brushed off the snow as she stood next to me and the bulk of it landed in my lap.

"Do you want me to make you eat dirt?" I challenged, narrowing my eyes.

Instead of reacting out of fear, which is what I was going for, Thistle merely snorted. "You're in a mood."

"She's completely in a mood," Mom agreed, unbothered by the fact that she was talking about me as if I wasn't even there. "I think it's because Brian is at the newspaper office today and tomorrow to pack up the rest of his stuff. Bay feels she can't be there, because it's uncomfortable for both of them."

"I'm right here," I reminded my mother.

"I could hardly forget." Mom gave my shoulder a sympathetic pat.

"You're channeling Aunt Tillie today, so it's not as if your personality is small enough to overlook."

Oh, well, that just did it. "That is the meanest thing you've ever said to me."

Thistle let loose with a smirk and a chuckle as she poured herself a mug of coffee and settled at the rectangular table. She was a few seats down from me – which I was convinced was on purpose so she could easily escape when she said something to irritate me – and she looked ready to start poking about in an effort to enrage. She definitely gets that from Aunt Tillie. I, on the other hand, am nothing like the woman. I'm not evil.

Yes, I'm a witch. I'm not a diabolical one, though. I leave that to Aunt Tillie and Thistle.

"You're clearly agitated," Thistle said after studying me for a beat. "Are you nervous about being the owner of the newspaper?"

I'd been getting this question from family members and people on the street ever since news went public that I was buying The Whistler, Hemlock Cove's lone newspaper. Brian Kelly was the grandson of the man who'd hired me, but the younger Kelly's efforts to turn The Whistler into something it wasn't – mainly a multimillion-dollar profit machine – failed. He finally tried to fire me, and the advertisers turned on him, resulting in me purchasing the newspaper (with a little help from my friends, family and boyfriend) while he prepared to slink out of town with nothing but a few thousand dollars and a chip on his shoulder.

Yeah, it wasn't exactly a comfortable environment at the office these days. I was still a week away from closing on the property thanks to an error in the initial paperwork. Brian refused to hang out anywhere else because he was keen to punish me for stealing his birthright. That's how he termed it once, mind you. I'm not the one who came up with that lovely complaint.

Wait ... what were we talking about again?

"I'm not nervous about owning the paper," I shot back. "I'm annoyed with Aunt Tillie. There's a difference."

"Oh, there's definitely a difference," Thistle agreed. "What did that old shrew do now?"

"Thistle!" Mom extended a warning finger. "You cannot talk about your great-aunt that way."

Thistle was blasé. She was used to Mom scolding her and didn't care in the least. In fact, now that she was living away from the family property and only visiting the inn our mothers owned a few times a week, her brashness had grown incrementally. "Why not? It's not as if she hasn't earned it."

"She's still your elder."

"Oh, did you just call her elderly?" Thistle's eyes flashed. "She won't like that."

"I most certainly didn't call her elderly," Mom shot back. She knew very well what Aunt Tillie would think about being called the E-word. To Aunt Tillie, that word was worse than every other word, including the C-word (which would be "crone" in this instance). It was only an option when she tried lying to the cops or getting out of jury duty. "If you even think of ... ."

Thistle didn't care to let Mom finish her threat, instead raising her voice so it would carry into the kitchen. "Did you hear that, Aunt Tillie? Winnie just called you 'elderly.' You should get out here and kick her butt."

Mom's eyes flashed. "You're in so much trouble," she hissed.

Thistle shrugged, unbothered. "She's also thinking of having T-shirts made up with a reminder that you're elderly so people won't forget. We're looking through the family albums to find a photograph of you now."

"I will kill you!" Mom was on her feet, her eyes trained on Thistle. "You are going to regret saying that." Instead of storming into the kitchen to deny the charge, Mom turned in the opposite direction and breezed through the door that separated the dining room from the rest of the inn.

I watched her go with a mixture of amusement and curiosity before turning my attention to a smug-looking Thistle. "That was mean."

"I'm fine with that."

"She'll make you pay."

"I'm fine with that, too." Thistle sipped her coffee. "I'm bored, so at least this will serve as a form of entertainment."

She had a point. "Is it still snowing?" I asked, shifting on my chair. "The weather forecaster is predicting at least a foot of snow overnight."

Thistle scowled. "Yeah, and it's getting rough out there. The road between town and the inn hasn't been plowed. It's almost impassable."

We live in northern Lower Michigan, so snow in January shouldn't be a big thing. That didn't mean it wasn't cause for concern occasionally. "Really?" I rolled my neck. "Landon is on his way over here right now. He's coming from Elk Rapids. Those side roads will be a mess."

Thistle took pity on me. "Don't worry about Landon. He's an FBI agent. He knows what he's doing. I'm sure he wouldn't risk the roads if he didn't think he could make it home."

In addition to being an FBI agent, Landon Michaels was my boyfriend ... and kind of my roommate ... and most definitely the person who made me smile the most. He'd moved into the family guesthouse, located on the edge of the property, several weeks before. Now that Thistle was preparing to move out and was spending more time with her boyfriend Marcus at what would soon be their new house, we had the run of the place. It was still a work in progress, but things had been going well.

"I'm sure he's fine, too." I forced a weak smile. "What are you doing here tonight? I would've thought you'd stick close to town rather than risk the roads."

"We're in a bind," Thistle explained, sobering. "The new furnace Marcus installed went out. He's not sure why, but he can't get in there to look at it until it warms up."

"Which means you're staying here for the night," I mused. It was early in the week, so The Overlook wasn't teeming with guests.

"I would've suggested staying with you at the guesthouse, but you've already turned my old room into your office," Thistle said dryly. "I don't want to return to the place where I've been so callously replaced."

There was no way I was rising to that bait. "You left."

"And you took over in five minutes flat."

"I created an office for myself," I clarified. "Landon took Clove's old room as his office and I took yours as mine. You knew it was going to happen."

"I did know it was going to happen. I just didn't know it was going to happen that quickly."

"We didn't really have a choice. With Brian walking around the newspaper office sighing and glaring all the time, I needed a place to work that wasn't under that roof."

"I get it." Thistle held up her hands. "I was just messing with you. What's Brian's deal, though? Why can't he just get out and leave you to it? It's as if he's dragging his feet."

"I think he's had second thoughts about the sale, but he knows better than to try to back out because he's afraid of Landon and Chief Terry," I explained. "Chief Terry kind of arranged for the sale to happen in the first place by rallying the shop owners when Brian tried to fire me. He's the reason I can buy the newspaper in the first place."

"He's a good guy." Thistle smiled. "I would've paid big money to see Brian's face when Chief Terry took him on. I bet he didn't even see it coming."

"I don't think Chief Terry was happy that day."

"Oh, I bet he was ticked." Thistle smiled at the thought. "I bet he made Brian's knees shake and there was probably a little bit of pee that shook loose. Chief Terry is a big guy, and Brian is a coward."

I made a face. "Yeah, let's not focus on the pee, shall we?"

Thistle chuckled. "It was just a thought." She leaned back in her chair and fixed me with a serious look. "Why do you look as if you're about to declare war?"

The question caught me off guard. "I'm perfectly calm."

"No, you're agitated. What were you doing when I got here?"

"Nothing."

"Bull. You were doing something."

"I don't know why I even bother to answer your questions when I know you're simply going to call me a liar," I grumbled. "You only believe what you want to believe."

"I also happen to know you," Thistle pointed out. "You're ticked off about something." She chewed her bottom lip as she debated. "You're angry with Aunt Tillie. I know that much. I caught that part of the conversation when I was coming in. What did she do to you?"

Now that was a loaded question. Aunt Tillie had done so many things to me over the course of my life that I'd lost count. "She's evil." I returned to my sulking with a glower on my face. "That woman is completely and totally evil."

Thistle chuckled, legitimately amused. "You're preaching to the choir, sister. I've been singing that particular song since I was six months old and learned how to speak."

I snorted. "You didn't learn to speak when you were six months old."

"I did so."

"You did not."

"I did so." Thistle's eyes flashed. "I was very advanced for my age."

"I'm older than you and was there," I reminded her. "You didn't start speaking when you were six months old. In fact, if I remember correctly, you didn't start until you were two, and instead spent an entire year grunting and pointing rather than talking because you were lazy."

Thistle furrowed her brow. "You take that back."

"It's the truth."

"Take it back anyway," Thistle barked.

"Fine. I take it back. You started talking at six months. You were a prodigy and we were all in awe."

"That's better." Thistle crossed her arms over her chest and stared me down. "I think you of all people should know that I had no choice but to start speaking early because I needed to protect myself – and therefore all of you as well – against Aunt Tillie."

"And speaking early did that for you?"

Thistle nodded without hesitation. "I didn't just speak. I uttered my first counter-curse. It was a powerful one, and that's how Aunt Tillie knew she'd met her match. I was a prodigy."

She was completely full of crap. Her first word had been "cookie" and I remembered very well because she was so delayed compared to Clove and me that everyone started clapping when she finally spit out the word. Twila (her mother) had been worried that Thistle was developmentally delayed, but it turned out she was simply lazy.

"I guess that's why you and Aunt Tillie have never gotten along," I drawled. "She's afraid of you because you're a prodigy."

"Exactly."

"Uh-huh." I pursed my lips. "You realize that I recognize you're full of crap, right?"

Thistle scorched me with a look. "Don't make me force you to eat dirt."

"There's too much snow outside to find dirt."

"Oh, I'll make an exception."

"Because you're a prodigy."

Thistle extended a warning finger. "If you keep this up, you'll be dead to me for the rest of the night."

"Why is that a concern? It's hardly the first time."

"Yes, but you need me," Thistle supplied. "You need me to help you plot against Aunt Tillie. I heard you whining when I got here. You want to mess with that old bat, but you need help doing it."

She wasn't wrong, still … . "What did you have in mind?"

This time the look that crossed Thistle's face was diabolical. "I'm so happy you asked."

Uh-oh. I'd clearly woken the beast. I tilted my head to the side, debating whether or not I cared that she was probably going to take things too far during our revenge plot. Ultimately I couldn't work myself up even a little at the prospect.

"What have you got in mind?"

"You're going to love this."

She was right. I loved it.

How awesome would it be to be able to send your kids up to the attic for five years and have them pop out as fully-functioning adults? That's how it works on soaps, and I think it sounds heavenly.

– Marnie after being stuck babysitting the girls for an entire weekend

TWO

It turned out that Thistle's plan wasn't genius as much as it was immature. Still, I was bored and worried about Landon being stuck on the frightening roads, so I agreed to help. By the time we were done, Thistle cast a spell that made Aunt Tillie feel as if there were ants in her pants – and infesting her chair. We were left with nothing better to do than to wait for Aunt Tillie to react and then ultimately slap back.

In the meantime, our other cousin Clove and her boyfriend Sam arrived. They looked a little worse for wear.

"We ended up in the ditch," Clove announced as she warmed her hands by the roaring fire in the dining room. "It's like Armageddon out there."

The simple statement caused my anxiety to escalate. "How did you get out?"

"I towed them out," Chief Terry announced as he strolled in the room. "I had my truck and a chain. We got lucky that they hadn't been in there more than a few minutes."

"I didn't even know you were here," I said, flashing a warm smile. Chief Terry was one of my favorite people – I even preferred him to most of my family members at times – and he would make a nice distraction while I tried not to obsess about the weather. "I'm glad you were there to save Clove and Sam."

"That makes two of us," Sam said, sitting at the table and pouring a mug of coffee. "I hate snow. Did I mention I hate snow?"

"That makes northern Lower Michigan a fabulous place for you to live," Thistle drawled, wrinkling her nose as she checked her phone. "Marcus is on his way." She flicked her eyes to her mother. "We'll need to stay here. I told you that, right? Our furnace is out."

Twila, who was all aflutter thanks to Chief Terry's presence, smiled. "It will be nice to have you with us tonight. We've missed seeing you as much as we used to." Her expression was fond as she touched Thistle's hair. "It will give us a chance to talk about what a stupid idea it was to dye your hair multiple colors."

Thistle scowled. "Oh, geez. I walked right into that one."

"You certainly did," Clove agreed, plopping herself on the floor and pushing her stocking-clad feet toward the fire. "I think we'll have to stay here, too. How many rooms do you have open?"

Clove's mother, Marnie, answered. "They're all open. Thankfully this happened early in the week. We have guests arriving Wednesday, but the roads should be cleared before then."

"Yes, we can be snowed in two full days together," Twila added enthusiastically.

Thistle's face at the suggestion was nothing short of hilarious. "That's a terrifying thought, isn't it?" She cast me a dubious look. "Still, you should stay here tonight, too. If we're all stuck ... it will be more fun if we're together."

"Oh, yay!" Clove clapped her hands. "I like that idea."

"You only like that idea because you want me to suffer as much as you guys," I groused. "It's not as if you want to spend that much time with your mothers."

"I heard that," Marnie warned. "Don't make me call your mother to deal with you."

"Where is my mother?" I craned my neck and stared through the opening that led to the lobby. "I haven't seen her in a bit. She took off because we were plotting against Aunt Tillie and I haven't seen her since."

"She's at the front desk balancing the books," Twila replied. "She always does that when she feels like the inn is closing in on her. That's her way of getting away from it all."

"It's only going to get worse when we start drinking," Thistle noted. "If she thinks this place feels small now, she hasn't seen anything yet."

"Good point." Marnie grinned as she poured Clove a mug of coffee and delivered it to her in front of the fire. "Still, I think it would be fun if everyone stayed here tonight. We have a big dinner planned and we can add a big breakfast." She offered up a saucy wink for Chief Terry's benefit. "That goes for you, too, Terry."

Even though he was often uncomfortable given the sustained interest from my mother and aunts – they were all vying for his attention – I had significant doubt that he would know what to do with any of them if one managed to land him. Of course, several weeks ago I pressed him on the issue and told him it was okay to make a choice. I was still waiting for him to select.

"I'd love to stay," Chief Terry said, taking me by surprise. "I don't think I have much of a choice. Getting back to town will be perilous. I hope people have the good sense to stay off the roads tonight."

That was about all I could take. I hopped to my feet. "I need to call Landon," I announced. "Maybe he can find a hotel close to wherever he's at. He shouldn't keep trying to get here. It's too far."

Chief Terry's expression softened. "You're worried. I should've realized that. Bay, Landon will be fine. He knows what he's doing."

"You just said that people shouldn't be on the roads."

"I didn't mean him."

"But ... ."

"Bay, he'll be fine." Chief Terry rested his big hand on my shoulder. "Don't get yourself in a tizzy."

"He's right," Thistle said pragmatically. "Do you see me freaking out because Marcus is still out there? No, because I have faith he knows what he's doing and that everything will be fine. You should try looking on the bright side of things."

I stared at her, convinced a second head was about to sprout. "Who are you and what have you done with my pessimistic cousin?"

"Ha, ha." Thistle rolled her eyes, snapping her head in the direction of the door when the sound of stomping footsteps filled the room.

I jerked my head in that direction and couldn't stop the disappointed roll of my stomach when I caught sight of Marcus. His shoulder-length hair was covered in snow, his cheeks flushed from the chill, and the look he shot Thistle was one of surprised pleasure when she launched herself at him.

"What's this?"

"I thought for sure you were dead in a ditch," Thistle announced, her voice shaky.

If I could've grabbed her around the neck and given her a good shake and gotten away with it I totally would've done it. There was every chance she can take me in a fair fight – and don't even get me going on an unfair fight, which she's prone to engage in regularly – so I wisely kept my mouth shut even as my anxiety doubled.

"It's nice to be loved." Marcus beamed as he gave Thistle a lingering hug. He knew very well her mood would shift to snarky and mean relatively quickly, so he took advantage of the situation while he could. "I was a little worried about getting here. The roads are a mess. Even when you're going slow and know where you're going it's a little frightening."

My stomach twisted as I chewed my bottom lip. "Maybe we should go looking for him." I glanced at Chief Terry. "Maybe ... ."

"Sweetheart, we don't know exactly where he is," Chief Terry reminded me gently. "He could be anywhere. Give it some time. If he's stopped someplace else because he feels that's the safest thing to do, you don't have to worry. He'll call. He wouldn't leave you suffering all night. That's not his way."

I knew that was true, yet ... . My heart hopped when I heard the front door open and I ran to the opening between rooms so I could get a glimpse of the action. Landon wasn't looking at me as he

AMANDA M. LEE

entered, but he said something to my mother that had both of them chuckling, his booming laughter filling the room.

Even though I knew it was ridiculous, I couldn't stop the relief from washing over me. Landon was here. He was safe. He would probably eat his weight in comfort food before the end of the night, but that was something to rejoice.

I opened my mouth to greet him, something schmaltzy on the tip of my tongue, but that was the moment Aunt Tillie made her presence known.

"What the ... ? Thistle! You'd better start running now. I know this was you."

Ah, the magical ants were doing their work. I spared a glance over my shoulder and locked gazes with Thistle. "That probably wasn't a good idea now that we're all stuck here for the night."

Thistle shrugged. "Don't worry. I've got it all under control."

That was a frightening thought. "How?"

"Watch." Thistle winked. "I didn't do it, Aunt Tillie," she called out. "It was Bay. You should put her on the top of your list."

My mouth dropped open as I realized what was happening. "You're dead to me," I seethed, my cheeks burning. "You're so dead they'll have to think of a new word for dead."

Thistle merely grinned. "Ah, it's good to spend time with family."

Something told me she wouldn't feel that way by the end of the night.

"HEY, SWEETIE."

Landon was all smiles when he strolled into the room. I did my best to pretend I hadn't been panicking about his safety and even managed to pull off a cool smile for about ten seconds ... and then I was on him.

"I was worried." I gave him a fierce hug. "You should've stopped at a hotel instead of braving the roads."

"Where were you?" Chief Terry asked.

"Elk Rapids. They had a big meth bust. I needed to sign paperwork, so I was there later than I wanted. The weather wasn't that bad when I left. By the time I got here, though, it was terrible. The last five miles between town and the inn took me almost forty-five minutes."

"Yeah, it's definitely nasty out there," Clove agreed. "By the way, we're all staying here for the night. That includes you and Bay. If you don't like it ... well ... suck it up."

Landon snickered. "You decide to be the bold one at the oddest of times."

"I have to be the bold one tonight. Thistle and Bay are on Aunt Tillie's list."

Landon's eyes lighted with amusement. "Oh, well, fun!" He kissed my forehead. "You need to unclench a bit, Bay. I'm fine. It was a rough ride, but I'm safe. Everyone is under one roof together, which I think is going to mean that things will get loud before the end of the night."

"Oh, you have no idea," Thistle intoned. "I already cursed Aunt Tillie to feel as if she has ants in her pants and then told her Bay did it. We're just getting started."

"Sounds fun." Landon smoothed my hair. "Do you think she'll whip out the bacon curse as retribution? If we're going to be snowed in, I can't think of a better way to pass the time."

"You want to spend the time sniffing your girlfriend?" Chief Terry's tone was dry. "I don't want to see that. In fact, I'm putting my foot down and demanding that no one gets cursed to smell like bacon. It might be a big inn, but it'll feel small once we've spent a few hours together."

"And we haven't even started drinking yet," Thistle added, sliding her eyes to the right when the dining room door swung open to allow Aunt Tillie entrance.

Describing Aunt Tillie isn't easy. She's four feet and eleven inches of pure mayhem. Tonight, for example, she wore St. Patrick's Day leggings, an oversized "I'm Here for the Boos" shirt and slippers with bunnies on them. Oh, and for the record, the bunnies looked stoned. Er, maybe they were meant to represent the rabbit from *Monty Python and The Holy Grail*. Yeah, that made more sense.

"There's the woman of the hour." Landon beamed as he released me. "If you're going to punish Bay, I want to request something that smells like bacon before the wine starts flowing. I figure if I get my request in early you'll be far more likely to take it into consideration."

Aunt Tillie shot Landon a withering look. "She won't smell like bacon when I'm done with her. I can promise you that."

Landon wasn't about to be deterred. "How about pot roast? That might be fun. Or ... wait ... we're snowed in." His eyes lighted with food delirium. No, honestly, he's a very food-oriented guy. "Chili. I love the smell of chili. Make her smell like chili and I'll give you three freebies on your pot field this summer."

Despite herself, Aunt Tillie was clearly intrigued by the suggestion. "Define 'freebie.'"

"I'll look the other way and not arrest you for illegally growing pot."

Aunt Tillie snorted. "You have no proof that I'm growing pot. You have a theory, which you can't back with facts. You'll have to do a lot better than that if you want me to make her smell like chili."

"You could split the difference and make her smell like a Coney dog," Thistle suggested. "If you add onions to the mix, it's bound to mess things up."

I scorched Thistle with the meanest look in my repertoire. "We're totally going to throw down once the chocolate martinis start flowing. You'd better prepare yourself."

"I'm looking forward to it."

I slid my eyes to Aunt Tillie and found her tilting her head to the side and pursing her lips. She looked pensive, which was never a good thing. "I don't want to smell like a chili dog."

"No one asked you." Aunt Tillie's gaze was pointed when it snagged with mine. "You're in big trouble, by the way. You've been nothing but a pain in the keister all afternoon."

"You spent the entire afternoon here?" Landon's expression was hard to read as he took a seat. "Why didn't you go to the newspaper office?"

"You know why."

Landon's lips curved downward. "Do you want me to talk to him?

I warned him once about giving you a hard time, but he's clearly not a fan of listening."

If I thought my relationship with Brian Kelly was testy, Landon's interactions with the man in question had been downright explosive the past few weeks. He was one insult away from punching my former boss in the face.

"Let it go," I instructed. "It's only another week. I can make it until then."

Landon didn't look convinced. "I don't want you suffering through his moods, Bay. It's not fair or right. You shouldn't be afraid to go into your own office."

"I agree with Landon," Aunt Tillie said, taking me by surprise. "You're being a big baby. Suck it up."

"That's not exactly what I said," Landon argued.

"Huh. That's what I heard." Aunt Tillie held up her hand to quiet Landon while remaining focused on me. "We're not done talking about this one whining all day. You totally ruined my afternoon."

"Then you shouldn't have said I was worse than Clove when it came to being a kvetch," I pointed out. "That's quite possibly the worst thing you've ever said to me."

Thistle snorted. "Not even close. Two weeks ago she said you were the rancid mayonnaise in a whiny sandwich. That's way worse than being a kvetch."

"She said I was a worse kvetch than Clove," I clarified. "I mean ... Clove!"

"That is bad," Thistle noted. "Things could be worse."

"You guys know I'm sitting right here, right?" Clove was furious. "It's going to be a long night if you keep this up."

"It's going to be a long night regardless," Aunt Tillie countered. "I was watching my stories. You know I don't like being interrupted when I'm watching my stories."

Landon cocked an eyebrow. "Stories?"

"Soap operas," Thistle supplied. "She loves soap operas. She used to make us watch them with her when we were little – even though they were beyond stupid – and I'm still traumatized by the experience."

"Watch it, mouth," Aunt Tillie warned, her expression serious. "You want to be very careful when you're talking about my stories."

Thistle snorted. "You made us watch that one where the guy had a twin brother hidden in his house and no one knew it. For like six straight months I thought we had people hidden in the basement."

"Everyone has secret twin brothers and sisters in Pine Valley," Aunt Tillie argued. "That show is gone, by the way. They've canceled almost all my stories. I only have four left and it's criminal, quite frankly. In fact … ." She turned to Landon. "Instead of arresting poor pot growers you should focus your attention on taking out the people who canceled my soaps. That would be a much better way for you to spend your time."

"I'll get right on that." Landon prodded me to sit in the open chair next to him, grabbing my hand and tracing his fingers over my palm. "Bay, I'm serious about this Brian Kelly situation. Maybe you should let me talk to him."

I opened my mouth to argue, but Aunt Tillie didn't give me a chance.

"Bay will handle her own issues with Brian Kelly. You don't always need to swoop in. She's perfectly capable of taking care of herself."

"I didn't say she wasn't," Landon countered. "I'm just … worried. He's getting progressively worse and he seems a bit unbalanced."

"And not in a fun way, like you, Aunt Tillie," Thistle added, grinning.

"You're definitely on my list," Aunt Tillie warned.

"I'll talk to him," Landon announced. He was clearly ignoring the other conversations bouncing around the room. "He needs a good warning."

"If you were in a soap opera, you'd throw a drink in his face and slap him around right about now," Aunt Tillie said. "That would be a lot more fun than whatever you're planning."

"Yes, well, we don't live in a soap opera," Landon said. "I know it feels as if we do sometimes, but we don't."

"Think about how much fun it would be if we did, though." Aunt Tillie's eyes momentarily sparkled, but she remembered where she was and quickly turned dour again when facing off with Thistle. "I would make you the person trapped in a well for months if this were a soap opera."

"And I would make you the person locked in a basement," Thistle fired back. "Our lives are close enough to soap operas. We don't need to make things worse."

She had a point. "So ... who wants to start drinking before dinner?" I asked, hoping to change the subject.

A bevy of hands shot into the air, including Chief Terry's.

"What?" he protested. "I can already see how this night is going to go. I want to numb myself appropriately."

He wasn't the only one. "Let's start with chocolate martinis and go from there."

"Now that sounds like a good idea," Landon enthused. "Now if only you smelled like chili while drinking your chocolate martini, all would be right in my world."

What kind of city has one serial killer, one mobster, one deranged doctor without a medical license running the hospital, the ancestor of a woman who wanted to freeze the world living on a nearby island named after a kitchen utensil, and a spy organization that doesn't handle any of these things? Seriously, I want to start my own crime ring and move there.

– Aunt Tillie on soap law enforcement strategies

THREE

I would like to say that we turned in early and drank only a respectable amount of liquor before realizing we didn't need alcohol to have a good time.

That's simply not how we roll.

We drank until things turned silly. Landon even decided we needed to try our hand at ballroom dancing at one point, spinning me around the lobby until we both laughed so hard I thought there was a chance we might wet ourselves.

Thistle and Aunt Tillie got into a spirited debate about soap operas, Aunt Tillie singing their merits while Thistle explained the absurdity of the genre. When Aunt Tillie wouldn't agree, Thistle gave up and started barking at her whenever our elderly great-aunt spoke. That, of course, set Aunt Tillie's teeth on edge and she started threatening curses.

I lost track of the conversation somewhere – probably when we started dancing – and by the time we found our way to our bedroom on the second floor it was midnight and we knew we were in for a rotten morning thanks to what was sure to be some rough hangovers. We would be snowed in, so we weren't too worried about it.

I woke with a start, the sunlight filtering through the window. I

AMANDA M. LEE

had a headache the size of the chip on Thistle's shoulder and I instantly reached for the bottle of aspirin I distinctly remembered leaving on the nightstand. It wasn't there. In fact, the nightstand in question didn't resemble the antique one I was sure I'd spied the evening before.

"Landon?" My tongue was thick, my throat dry.

Landon didn't move. "Shh."

I thought about letting him sleep. He was crabby when he had a hangover. Heck, we both were. Still, something was definitely wrong. I didn't think there was any way to save him from it, so letting him escape in slumber was a wasted effort. Plus, well, I didn't want to deal with it alone.

What? I have a hangover. I can't be giving and selfless when I feel as if there's an alien inside my brain and it's knocking really loudly in an attempt to escape. It's simply impossible.

"Landon."

"Sweetie, I love you dearly, but if you don't lower your voice I'm going to have to get my own room."

I was barely talking in a rasp – trust me, I couldn't take my voice on full volume either – so I knew he was in rough shape. "Landon, I don't want to alarm you, but ... it's morning."

"We're snowed in. We can sleep all day."

"Yes, but ... the thing is ... um ... ." I had no idea how to broach the obvious problem. You would think after being shoved into Aunt Tillie's memories, a fairy tale world and even the future I would know how to tell Landon we'd been transported to an alternate reality ... again. I recognized the truth instinctively when I saw the nightstand – there's no way my mother would have a marble nightstand with pearl accents, for crying out loud – and I figured Aunt Tillie had gotten her revenge after all.

"Shh. Sweetie, we're snowed in. We can't often say that. I have the day off. You have the day off. Let's spend the day in bed ... but let's make it a quiet day, at least to start."

Even though my head throbbed thanks to my personal choices

from the previous evening I was strong enough to take offense. "Quiet day, huh?"

"I still love you." Landon absently patted the spot between us. "I just really need you to be quiet."

I licked my lips as I stared at him for a long moment, annoyed. "Fine." I tossed off the covers and stood, taking my first gander at the new room. The decorations were ornate, bordering on garish. It was as if someone took a catalog from the most expensive furniture store in existence and opted to purchase every item they could ... whether it matched or not. "It's almost as if *Dynasty* and *Miami Vice* met, had a drunken one-night stand, and then made a baby."

"We'll watch *Miami Vice* later," Landon murmured.

"Yeah, yeah." His disinterest agitated me. I headed toward the bathroom to my left and, after giving the tacky bathroom the once over I rummaged in the medicine cabinet until I came up with aspirin and filled one of the glasses next to the sink with water. I popped the tablets, downed all the water and then refilled it. After the second glass of water, the leading edge of the dehydration was gone and I could actually stand to look at myself in the mirror. Surprisingly, it wasn't a horrifying sight. I looked relatively clear-eyed and awake, a small miracle all things considered.

"Holy crap! Where are we?" Landon's voice was like nails on a chalkboard.

I moved to the doorway, smirking when I saw the look on his face. He was bare-chested, his black hair wild from a night of hard sleep, and his eyes were full of incredulity as he looked around the room.

"Good morning, sunshine," I drawled. "Welcome to another nightmare brought to us by Aunt Tillie. Fasten your seatbelt and enjoy the ride."

Landon's expression was dark when he swiveled. "Do you think this is funny?" His eyes were so red from the hangover that he almost looked possessed. "This is pretty far from funny, Bay. In fact ... nope. I'm not doing it. She can't win if I refuse to play."

I watched as he pulled the comforter over his head and dived beneath the covers, a small smile playing at the corners of my lips. He tossed and turned, reminding me of an agitated bed bug with attitude, as he tried to get comfortable.

I decided to approach him carefully. "Landon."

"Nope. I was serious. I'm not playing."

"Fair enough." I knew he wouldn't stick to his claim. For now he needed to feel as if he was in control, though. "There's aspirin. Would you like some?"

Landon jerked down the comforter so I could see the top of his head. "How do you know it's not cursed aspirin?"

"I took three tablets myself. I'm fine."

"You're not fine, Bay. You're trapped in another nightmare. You have no idea what's going to happen. We could be in the past. We could be in the future. If it's the future and Aunt Tillie is hanging around with the pope again, by the way, I'm totally going to become an atheist ... or one of those people who preps for the end of the world. Oh, yeah, that's what I'm going to do. Get ready for the end of the world."

He was ranting. He couldn't seem to stop himself. "So ... where did we land on the aspirin?"

Landon heaved out a groan. "Fine. I'll risk the cursed aspirin."

Somehow I knew he'd say that. I delivered the aspirin and water, pursing my lips as he downed both. When he was done, he seemed a bit calmer ... although only marginally.

"Where are we this time?" Landon asked, resigned.

"I don't know." I gestured toward the ornate mirror on the wall. "It's like we're living in a bad eighties movie or something. I can't think of another way to describe it."

"Why would she send us to the eighties?"

I shrugged. "That always was her favorite fashion era."

"Yeah, I should've seen that coming."

"I'm not sure this is the eighties," I cautioned. "It merely reminds me of the eighties."

"Does it really matter?" Landon rested against the pillows. "We don't have to play, Bay. She'll let us out eventually. She'll have no choice. We can spend the entire day in here ... in this eighties bedroom ... and spend alone time together. We don't have to look out there and see what horrible things she has planned for us."

It was a thought, although it wasn't one I was particularly fond of entertaining. "We'll get out faster if we play."

"You don't know that. We haven't refused to play yet. We have no idea what will happen if we don't engage with her ridiculous stories."

He had a point, still ... . "I'm going to look around. You can stay here. I'll come back and tell you what's going on when I have a better idea. You can make your decision then."

Landon was incredulous. "Do you really think I'm going to do that?"

I shrugged. "No, but I think you need to work yourself up to play this go around. It won't hurt for you to rest while I look around and then report back."

Landon's expression was grim. "I'm not playing." He was stubborn under the best of circumstances. He obstinately grabbed the remote control from the nightstand on his side of the bed and clicked on the television. The volume was high and caused me to jolt as a voice – a voice that was oddly familiar – started to speak.

"Previously on *All My Witches* ... ."

Uh-oh.

"What's this?" Landon furrowed his brow as he stared at the television screen.

The announcer's voice droned on.

"Jericho Steele, an undercover police officer, continued to work his case even as danger closed in at every turn."

"Son of a ... that's me!" Landon jabbed at the television. "Look at that. It's me."

As if drawn by something outside of myself, I sat on the end of the bed and focused on the television. The man on the screen was clearly Landon, although he was dressed much differently and apparently had trouble keeping his shirt on ... at least if the montage was to be believed.

"This isn't good," I muttered.

Landon was beside himself. "Oh, what was your first clue?"

I ignored the sarcasm and kept my attention trained on the television. The voice reminded me of my mother, and I was certain Aunt Tillie did that on purpose.

"Jericho's biggest problem isn't the mobster who wants to kill him; it's the woman who has stolen his heart." Someone who looked remarkably like me – although with a much more expensive and impractical wardrobe – appeared on the screen. "Echo Waters is a former model, current artist, possible bar owner and potential philanthropist who married an evil man. Michael Ferrigno is a mobster known for three things: his charisma, his ruthless ambition and his pretty if conflicted wife. Oh, yeah, he's also known for his rather impressive dimples."

Landon snorted. "She named you Echo Waters. That is just ... mean."

"Laugh it up, Jericho," I muttered.

"Soap opera names are stupid."

He wasn't wrong. I rolled my neck until it cracked and continued watching.

"Jericho is determined to bring down Ferrigno no matter who gets hurt in the process. Unfortunately for Jericho, he might not be able to follow through on his promise because his love for Echo runs deep ... really deep, like to the tips of his toes deep. Like if there were giant sharks living in hidden trenches at the deepest part of the ocean, we're talking that deep."

"Oh, geez." Landon slapped his hand to his forehead. "This is unbelievable."

I lifted my finger to silence him, intent on the television.

"Joining Echo and Jericho on their journey are Cora Devane, a former spy and current fashion designer who married for money and now suffers for love," the voice said as Thistle's image appeared on screen. Her husband looked like an extra from *Cocoon* he was so old and wrinkly. "Cora never loved Dominic Woods, but that's okay because she gets her thrills with his son, Darko Woods."

I wasn't surprised when Marcus appeared in a scene with Thistle. His handsome features looked right at home on a soap opera.

"Wait, Thistle is married to the old dude, but sleeping with his son, who just happens to be Marcus?" Landon was baffled. "That sounds about right. Wait ... did she say his name was Darko Woods? Like Dark Woods? Who picks soap opera names? I mean ... seriously."

"I don't know." I was fascinated by the story playing out on the television, so I couldn't spare much effort for Landon's disgust. "Let me watch."

"Cinder Cramer could be friend or foe – nobody knows – because she's never one thing on any given day," the television voice explained. "She's from a rich family, yet earns her money in a variety of different ways. She's a naughty nurse by day and a steamy waitress by night, stripping for tips at the local dive bar when she wants extra money."

"Oh, Clove won't like this," I muttered when I recognized the dark-haired woman cavorting on screen.

"Of course, it's not Cinder's fault," the voice continued. "That's what happens when you have multiple personalities and only one body for them all to share."

"Multiple personalities?" Landon was flummoxed. "Is that really a thing?"

I shrugged, noncommittal. "It depends on who you ask," I replied. "Some people think it's real. Some don't. It's a regular fixture on soaps, though."

"Oh, well, good. I thought things would be boring otherwise."

I ignored his sarcasm and pointed at the screen. "It's not done."

"Cinder isn't alone in her struggle. She has the love of a good man to help her ... that is when he's not helping Ferrigno with his criminal empire. Cane Wharton is a famous attorney who survives off the proceeds he makes from defending Ferrigno – even though the guilt is almost too much for him to bear – but he follows his true heart's desire when he has the time. That means long shifts in the hospital where he volunteers his free time as a brain surgeon on weekends."

This time the laugh Landon let loose with was so loud it caused me to jerk my shoulders. "He's a criminal attorney during the week and a brain surgeon on weekends? Who comes up with this stuff?"

"If you watch soaps, you know that you have to suspend disbelief,"

I explained. "Aunt Tillie used to have us watch with her all the time when we were kids. She'd get really into it."

"Did you like it?"

I shrugged. "The guys were hot."

"Now they're really hot." Landon pointed to his image on the screen. "I'm like the hottest soap hero ever, huh?"

"You're not bad."

"Not bad." Landon moved closer, poking me in the side to cajole a smile. Apparently he was feeling better. In fact, he seemed to be enjoying himself. Unfortunately for him, I didn't expect the feeling to last.

I opened my mouth to tease him, fully embrace the light mood, but I didn't get the chance because the television was talking again.

"Pulling all the strings in the quiet hamlet of Camelot Falls is Alexis Kane," the voice intoned. "She's more than the mother of a mobster. She's more than the smartest woman in town. She's more than the most powerful being on the planet. She's ... everything."

"Oh, I bet I know who Alexis is," Landon growled.

I knew, too, and we were both right. Aunt Tillie's face swam into view. She wore a bejeweled floor-length gown with blue accents, more makeup than I'd seen her wear during the course of her life, and a gleaming tiara that boasted what looked to be real diamonds.

"This isn't going to be good," I said.

"No." Landon linked his fingers with mine. Perhaps he wanted to make me feel better. Maybe he wanted to make himself feel better. Probably it was a little of both. He anchored himself to me, and we watched the rest with unfettered awe.

"Alexis is a mother first and a megalomaniac second," the voice said. "While she's anxious and capable when it comes to her son's business, she's more interested in her scientific endeavors."

"Scientific endeavors?" Landon was beyond amused. "Why do I picture those geeks in *Ghostbusters*?"

Oddly, that sounded about right.

"Alexis is keeping her big plan to herself, but those in the know are terrified of her power and fury," the voice said. "What does she have planned? It's anyone's guess, but right now her main goal is to finish construction of her freezing ray."

"Freezing ray?" Landon's shoulders shook with unconstrained laughter. "Now it's veering into comic book territory."

"The freezing ray will be aimed at her enemies – and that list is almost endless – but her ultimate goal is to control the world's water supply," the voice continued. "If she can freeze the water before delivering it, she'll be able to unleash her ultimate weapon ... the snow sharks of doom."

"Oh, that did it." Landon swung his legs over the side of the bed. "She can't be serious with this one."

Sadly, I had a feeling she was completely serious ... and that was before Aunt Tillie appeared on the screen. It was a close-up of her face, the blue eyeshadow so garish that it reminded me of a mutant Smurf. She opened her mouth to speak, and that's when I knew we were in a very special world.

"I'll get you if it's the last thing I ever do," Aunt Tillie cackled, her eyes locking with mine through the screen. "You're all on my list."

So he's a mobster and everyone is afraid of him, yet from all I can tell the only thing he does is throw bar glasses and knock up every woman he sees. Am I missing something? And, by the way, I totally want to be a soap opera mobster. They get all the play.
– Landon watching an episode with Bay during a lazy afternoon

FOUR

I was still sorting through my flabbergasted feelings when the television blinked off.

"Snow sharks? I just ... this is worse than anything she's ever put us through," Landon lamented.

"She was watching a movie on the SyFy channel the other day and it had snow sharks," I explained, my mind busy. "She thought it was a cool idea and was trying to figure out a way to militarize them to terrorize Mrs. Little. She thought she had a legitimate chance of marooning her inside her house for the entire winter."

"But why would a soap opera care about stuff like that? They're supposed to be about love in the afternoon, right?"

"Yes and no. Soaps are more than just music montages and hot sex scenes."

"I always thought they were all about romance and kids dying so the women who play their mothers have an opportunity to cry for daytime Emmys and stuff."

"That happens. There's a lot of action, too. Believe it or not, freezing the world was an actual thing on *General Hospital* in the eighties."

"How do you know that? You would've been a little kid in the late eighties."

"Yeah, but Aunt Tillie got really excited when Soapnet was a thing back in the day and they ran reruns," I explained. "We watched them with Aunt Tillie ... especially during the winter when there was nothing to do. The freezing the world storyline was a big thing."

"Okay, I'm going to refrain from telling you what I think about that story, because it has no bearing on our situation, but what does she expect us to do in this world?"

"What do you mean?"

"Well, all the other places she's sent us have had lessons rolled into the stories," Landon replied. "The fairy tale world was about overcoming obstacles while also keeping us busy so she could illegally sell her wine. The time we got stuck in her memories was an accident, but you still learned a lot about your family – and especially her – in the process.

"The Christmas story, however annoying, was about making sure we appreciated family," he continued. "What are we going to learn in a soap opera world?"

That was a very good question. "I don't know. She could simply be punishing us because we made fun of soap operas last night ... and cast that little spell that made her itchy all over. She definitely wasn't happy about that."

"No, but she always has several reasons for doing the things she does."

"So ... what do you think her plan is?" I challenged. "You've known her a long time now. You've been put through the wringer thirty different ways. What do you think she wants?"

"I don't know. I don't know her like you do."

I scratched my head as I considered how to respond. "I don't know what she has planned, but it's bound to be all kinds of messed up. I know your initial reaction is to stay here, but I think if we do that we'll simply be delaying the inevitable. Eventually she'll force us into the world she created if only because she wants us to see all the work she put into it."

Landon's expression was unreadable. "So you think we should play the game."

"I don't think she'll let us do anything else."

Landon ran his tongue over his teeth. "Okay. Let's do this."

His change of heart was surprising. "Really?"

"We might as well." Landon flashed a sheepish grin as he hopped to his feet. "I've always fancied myself a leading man. I thought it would be in an action movie and not on a soap opera, but what could possibly happen that's so bad?"

WE SHOWERED AND DRESSED because it seemed to be the thing to do. I don't know what I was expecting, but the house I found myself in was so obscenely large it reminded me of a fairy tale castle rather than a soap opera mansion.

"Look at this place." Landon shook his head as he stared at the ornate ceiling. It boasted a painted mural featuring men in loincloths dancing around a fire. "Who would live in a house like this?"

"Something tells me that Aunt Tillie has gone to a lot of effort to make this world as ridiculous as possible. If we thought the future she plotted out for us was unbelievable, just wait. Soaps are already ridiculous. She's going to take the basics and run with them … and it's going to be all kinds of ugly."

"Bay!"

I jerked at the sound of my name, swiveling to find Thistle, Clove, Marcus and Sam stalking toward us. They were overdressed – just like us – and they didn't look happy.

"Speaking of ugly." Landon made a clucking sound with his tongue. "Look at Clove's shirt. It looks as if half of it was designed by one person and the other half by someone else."

"She has multiple personalities in this world," I reminded him. "Aunt Tillie probably wants to remind us of it."

"Oh, well, I can't wait to meet her other personalities," Landon muttered. "I'm sure they'll be all sorts of crazy."

"I'm sure you're exactly right."

Thistle's face was red with fury – and her hair was a dull dirty blond, bordering on boring brown, that I hadn't seen since she was fourteen. "Do you know what that evil witch has done?"

I nodded. "I saw the recap for *All My Witches* when we were still in our room. Landon was considering hiding in there, but we figured it was better to face the music rather than try to wait it out."

"That's what we decided, too," Clove said. "We thought it might take forever to get out of here if we did nothing. Of course, when I suggested it, Sam thought it was one of my other personalities talking. He's a lawyer and a brain surgeon, so he decided he should be in charge this time."

I pursed my lips to keep from laughing at Sam's hangdog expression. It was fairly obvious that he and Clove had gone at each other about their backstories.

"Hey, we might need a brain surgeon before the day is out," Landon said. "I have an incredible urge to beat my head against the wall rather than sit back and figure out what this world has to offer. I figure it might be less painful."

"Oh, now, don't be a baby," Thistle chided. "You're an undercover police officer in love with your mark. Your story isn't terrible."

"Speaking of marks ... ." Marcus tilted his chin toward the end of the hallway where a tall man boasting deep dimples that I remembered from the clip reel stared in our direction.

"Who is that?" Clove asked. "He looks familiar."

"Maybe one of your other personalities is involved with him," Sam suggested.

"No, he's the one married to Bay's character." Landon's voice was positively dripping with disdain. "Look at that guy. He's like a stereotypical mobster. He's got slicked-back hair and everything."

"He's a lot hotter than most mobsters I've seen in movies and television," Clove argued. "In fact ... ." She didn't get a chance to finish because the man, Michael Ferrigno, was on us and apparently interested in claiming the woman he believed to be his wife.

"There you are!" Michael grabbed both sides of my face and planted a long, hot and lingering kiss on my mouth. If I wasn't so surprised by the move I might've taken a moment to enjoy it – he was quite talented in that department and didn't suffer from wandering tongue syndrome – even though I was dedicated to Landon beyond all else.

"Hey!" Landon shoved his hand between Michael and me and tugged me backward. "Watch your hands, man!"

For his part, Michael seemed amused more than anything else. "She's my wife, Jericho, which you very well know. That means she's my property. My hands belong on my property."

"Yeah, I wouldn't say that again if you don't want three feet slamming into your groin," Landon said pointedly. "As for the rest ... just don't do it. I don't think your wife feels all that well, and she's probably not in the mood for your vigorous brand of kissing. Isn't that right, Bay?"

"Who is Bay?" Michael asked, confused.

"Echo," Thistle automatically corrected. "He meant Echo. He gets confused easily. I think it's from all the blows he's taken to the head. He's one of your henchmen, right?"

Landon made an exaggerated face. "I don't think he uses the word 'henchman.'"

Michael shook his head. "No, I do. That's what it said on your application right before your interview."

"Really?" Landon cocked a dubious eyebrow. "I filled out an application to serve as one of your ... henchmen?"

"How else would you get the job?" Michael turned his quizzical expression to me. "How are you, my darling? You look quite fetching today, although I can't say I wasn't a bit surprised when I woke up alone. Where did you spend your night?"

"Oh, well ... ."

"She was with me," Clove answered automatically. "We were hanging out."

"At the strip club?" Michael made a face. "I've warned you about hanging out at the strip club, darling. You'll get a bad reputation."

"Right, because being married to a mobster is so good for her reputation," Landon muttered.

Michael ignored the sarcasm. "I have a job for you, Jericho."

"He's talking to you," Sam helpfully offered Landon.

Landon shot him a withering look. "I got it. What's the job?"

"I need you to get the thing."

Landon waited for him to expand on his instructions, but Michael seemed to think that was enough for Landon to figure out what he should be doing.

"The thing?"

"Yes, you know about the thing. We've talked about it at length."

I yelped when I felt someone pinch my rear end, jerking to the side and crashing into Landon. "What the ... ?"

"Oh, don't act cagey, my little crème brulèe," Michael teased. "I know you really like it when I ... touch you there."

Landon's eyebrows practically flew off his forehead. "Where did you touch her?" He turned to me, his expression murderous. "Where did he touch you?"

"Why do you even care?" Michael challenged, his demeanor breezy. "She's my wife."

"No, she's not," Landon snarled.

"Dude, you're supposed to be playing the game," Marcus whispered. "I don't think you're doing it right."

"Shut up," Landon barked. He grabbed my arm and drew me back so Michael wasn't close enough to accidentally – or purposely, for that matter – brush against me. "Don't touch her."

"She's my wife."

"Stop saying that."

I lifted my hands to stave off a potential fight. "Can we get back to the thing? I think Jericho needs a reminder of what the thing is."

Michael rolled his eyes so hard it was a wonder he didn't tip to the side. "What do you think the thing is?"

"Well ... ." Landon looked to me for help.

Michael was a mobster. That could mean he had his fingers in a great many of nefarious pies. I latched onto the first one that passed through my mind. "Drugs. You want him to pick up a ... bag of drugs, right?"

Landon's expression was incredulous. "A bag of drugs?"

"You know I don't run drugs, darling," Michael admonished. "My brother died from a drug overdose, and I've sworn off the practice. How could you forget that?"

"Oh, well, that's a terrible story," Clove offered. "I think it's great that you don't run drugs. Drugs are terrible. They rip apart families and break hearts."

"How do you know?" Thistle challenged.

Clove's eyes flashed. "I've seen it on television."

"Right."

"Maybe it's a prostitute," Sam suggested. "Mobsters run prostitution rings, right?"

The look Michael scorched Sam with was straight out of a Francis Ford Coppola movie. "My sister was tricked into prostitution by an older man who took advantage of her. She died after taking the wrong trick to a bad hotel. I do not engage in prostitution."

Sam swallowed hard at the expression on Michael's face. "Good to know."

Landon sighed to silence them. "So the thing isn't drugs or prostitution. I'm guessing it's stolen goods then. Do I need to pick up a shipment or something?"

"Stolen goods?" Michael made a tsking sound, disappointment positively rolling off of him. "I would never deal in stolen goods. I believe in being honorable. You don't steal things if you're honorable. Besides, I had a brother who was killed during a home invasion robbery. I honor his legacy by not dealing in stolen goods."

"It sounds dangerous to be one of your siblings," Thistle noted.

"It is dangerous to be in this world," Michael corrected.

"So if we're not dealing with stolen goods or drugs, how about garbage contracts?" Landon suggested.

"Garbage contracts?" Sam wrinkled his nose. "What does that have to do with anything?"

"Everyone knows that garbage companies are full of mobsters," Thistle supplied.

"That's true." Clove was somber. "We saw it on television the other night. A lot of politicians are losing their jobs down south because they were bribed by garbage contractors."

"Oh, well, that's just … a smelly thought," Sam complained.

"It's not garbage contracts." Michael's agitation was beginning to show. "You know what the thing is. I'm not telling you in front of a group of people … especially my lawyer."

"Of course not." Landon clenched his fists. "Okay. Fine. I'll get the thing."

"Great." Michael's smile was back in place. "While you're doing that … ." He reached out his fingers and touched the hem of my shirt. "I missed you last night, my darling. I have some time free this morning if you would like to get … reacquainted." Michael offered a saucy wink that turned my stomach. He was handsome, in a disarming way, and the dimple was utterly adorable. He made me queasy, though. Plus, well, he was extremely touchy-feely.

"Oh, well, I have an appointment," I lied, searching my mind for something to offer that he would buy.

"A photo shoot?"

I was understandably confused. "Photo shoot?"

"You're a model," Thistle reminded me. "I'm guessing that's what you do, just sit around and pose for photos."

That didn't sound terrible. "Right. Um, yeah. I have a photo shoot."

"Why do you get to be a model?" Clove complained. "I always thought I should be the one to be a model."

"You're not even five feet tall," Thistle shot back. "You can't be a model. You're a miniature horse instead of a giraffe. That's not how it works."

Clove balked. "I could be a great model. I could do it professionally."

"You're a stripper," Michael offered. "That's close to a model."

"Don't bring that up," Clove warned. "I'm offended that Aunt Tillie would even include that tidbit in her horrible game."

I didn't blame Clove. She really had gotten an "out there" story. In the grand scheme of things, I'd gotten off light.

"I'm going to my photo shoot," I said. "I'll be back … later."

"That's fine." Michael had seemingly moved on from his determination to spend quiet (or maybe not so quiet) married time with me. "I have very important meetings at the warehouse."

"That's good." Landon forced a smile for Michael's benefit. "You should definitely go to the warehouse. Just out of curiosity, what do you house in the warehouse if you don't run drugs or stolen goods?"

"You know."

"No, I don't."

"Yes, you do."

"No, I don't."

Landon flicked his eyes to me. "This world makes no sense. What kind of mobster doesn't do anything illegal yet calls himself a mobster?"

I shrugged. "How should I know? I don't even know what a real mobster does."

"He kills people like Jimmy Hoffa," Clove replied.

"Oh, well, that answers that question." I pressed the heel of my hand to my forehead. This world was already tiresome, and figuring out the rules was daunting. "Let's just get out of here. We'll go find the thing and go on from there."

"I thought you were going to a photo shoot," Michael challenged.

"I am. You must have misheard me."

"Oh, it happens." Michael leaned forward and pinched my butt a second time, causing me to yelp. "I already miss you."

Landon was unbelievably close to losing his temper. "Don't do that again!"

"She's my wife," Michael fired back. "I can do whatever I want to her."

"No, you can't. In fact … ."

Marcus put a hand on Landon's chest to keep him from throwing himself at Michael. "You'll be playing into Aunt Tillie's game if you do that. She expects you to pick a fight. Let's get out of here. We'll find the thing and take a look around. We need to explore if we're going to figure out how to get out of here."

Landon's chest heaved as he debated the logic behind Marcus' words. Finally he blew out a sigh. "Fine. If he does it again, though, I'm totally breaking his hand."

"If he does it again, I'll help you."

Michael, who was doing a bang-up job of pretending he wasn't listening, reached out with his hand, causing me to shrink back from his busy fingers, but Thistle wisely slapped it away.

"You are the dumbest mobster ever," Thistle said. "How did you even get the job?"

Michael pointed at his dimples. "You wouldn't believe what these can accomplish."

"Well, at least you know who you are."

"And we need to know where we're going," Landon said. "Let's get out of here. I don't ever want to see this house again."

So let me get this straight ... she's pregnant with twins, but they each have different fathers? This sort of smut shouldn't be allowed on television. I warned you girls about doing stuff like this, right? It's how you get a reputation ... and not a good one like I have. This is demented. It's wrong. It's so stupid. It's ... who is he? He's hot. I like him. This show is absolutely wonderful.

– Twila on soap ethics

FIVE

"I don't like that guy."

Landon clutched my hand so tightly as we left the mansion that I thought he might break off my fingers.

"Oh, suck it up, big guy," Thistle chided. "We have bigger things to worry about than your testosterone-fueled ego."

Landon shot her a dark look. "Excuse me?"

Thistle refused to back down. "You heard me. You don't seem to understand how soap operas work, and that's a detriment to us in this world. You need to get with the program."

"He pinched her butt ... twice!"

"Like Bay hasn't had her butt pinched in the real world," Thistle argued. "You need to let it go. We have other things to worry about."

"Like what?"

"You saw the footage reel," I interjected. "Aunt Tillie wanted us to see it. She wanted us to understand the rules."

"What rules?" Landon's temper flared. "As far as I can tell, this world has no rules."

"It doesn't have much logic," Thistle corrected, "but as for rules ... it has rules. For example, in this world Bay is married to a mobster, but she's having an affair with you. You're an undercover cop working to bring down Bay's husband. How do you think that's going to end?"

"With me winning," Landon answered without hesitation. "If he pinches her butt again, I'll pinch his head off his neck."

"Yeah, yeah." Thistle waved off Landon's threat and focused on me. "She's going to use every soap trope in her arsenal. You spent more time with her watching soaps as a kid than I did. What were her favorites?"

Oh, well, that was an interesting question. "I don't know. She liked the wacky ones."

"Why doesn't that surprise me?" Landon muttered, rolling his eyes to the sky.

"Which wacky ones?" Thistle pressed.

"I don't remember. There was one about an alien."

"An alien?" Landon was beside himself. "Why would a soap opera have aliens?"

"Dude, you need to stop saying 'soap opera' that way," Clove snapped. "The longer you're derogatory about the genre, the more likely Aunt Tillie is to punish you beyond belief in this world. It will be much worse than Bay getting her butt pinched."

"She's right," I added. "You don't understand soap operas. I'm not sure we do ... at least not like Aunt Tillie. She's going to throw everything she's got at us. We need to be ready."

Landon pressed the heel of his hand to his forehead. "Fine. You know more about what we're going to face. What's up first?"

"The thing."

"What thing?"

"Whatever thing Michael wants us to find," I replied. "We have to figure out what it is. It's very clearly part of the story."

"I don't really care about Michael's thing," Landon shot back.

"I thought he was handsome," Clove announced, offering up a mischievous smile. "What is it with those dimples? What kind of mobster has dimples like that?"

"He's not a real mobster," Landon argued. "I mean ... how does he make his money? He doesn't run drugs or move stolen merchandise.

He doesn't organize prostitution rings and employ pimps. How does he make his money?"

"You don't understand," I challenged. "In this world he's supposed to be a bad guy, but you root for him anyway. You're not supposed to know what terrible things he does, because that makes rooting for him more difficult. It happens all the time on soaps."

"Whatever." Landon crossed his arms over his chest and stared across the empty highway. There was absolutely no vehicle traffic, and it looked to be something of a condensed area. The mega-mansion was practically on top of the highway, which wasn't exactly aesthetically pleasing. I couldn't think too much about that, because I had other things to worry about.

"Okay, what kind of thing could a mobster want?" Clove adopted a pragmatic tone. "Maybe it has something to do with whatever business he really does. We should've hung around long enough to figure out what that was."

"Please, if Michael pinched Bay's butt one more time Landon was going to kill him, and then we would've found out what kind of jails they have in soap opera world," Sam countered. "I think we're better off figuring this out on our own."

"But what could it be?" Clove rubbed her forehead. "I just ... I can't think what a soap opera mobster would possibly want us to retrieve."

"It's not about what he wants us to find," Thistle corrected. "It's about what Aunt Tillie wants us to find."

"Why do you say that?" Marcus asked. "Why would it be about what Aunt Tillie wants?"

"Because she plays his mother in this reality, although her age means she should really be his grandmother, but we'll let that slide," Thistle replied. "These curses are always about Aunt Tillie. They're about what she wants and propping up her ego.

"We shouldn't be thinking about what Michael wants," she continued. "We should be thinking about what Aunt Tillie wants. She'll simply bend the storyline to fit her needs."

"That's smart thinking." I scratched the back of my neck. "The little preview clip said Aunt Tillie had her fingers in a lot of pies, but her ultimate goal was to freeze the world so she could bring forth a group of mutant snow sharks. So, what item – or rather, items – would Aunt Tillie need to freeze the world?"

"A death ray?" Landon was feeling snarky. "Don't you use a death ray to freeze the world?"

"No, you use diamonds," Sam answered, taking everyone by surprise with his certainty. "Every time I've ever seen anyone build a freezing ray in books, movies or television, they've used diamonds. They used diamonds in the Batman comics and movies for Mr. Freeze. They used diamonds in *Buffy the Vampire Slayer*. That's always the answer in everything I've ever seen."

"Diamonds, huh?" I racked my brain. "Okay, that's a place to start. Where would someone in a soap world keep diamonds?"

"How about in the lost city of Zeton?" Landon asked.

I knit my eyebrows. "Zeton? Where is Zeton?"

Landon pointed across the way to where a large billboard sat next to an over-sized door, which was cut into the wall of what could only be described as a really lame mountain. Clove read the billboard out loud.

"Welcome to the lost city of Zeton. We make the future look like the past. Get away from it all and embrace a whole new set of problems. And, oh, we have diamonds here."

"Well, that's a subtle billboard," Thistle said, making a face. "It's as if she drew us a map."

"Soaps are never subtle," I pointed out. "She did draw us a map. She clearly wants us to go to Zeton next."

Landon let loose a dramatic sigh. "I know I'm starting to sound like a broken record here, but why would a soap opera have a lost city under a mountain? That's science fiction."

"I keep telling you that what you believe about soap operas isn't true," I argued. "They're much more complex than you're giving them credit for. Now, I won't pretend they always make sense or you don't have to swallow your disbelief to get into them, but they're more than just people kissing during music montages.

"Soaps sometimes handle big stories, like AIDS and rape," I continued. "They do absurd things. You need to prepare yourself, because I have a feeling we'll be dealing with a lot of crazy scenarios."

"My life has been a crazy scenario since I met you," Landon grumbled.

I knew he didn't mean the comment as a jab, but I took it that way all the same. "I know I should probably apologize for this happening to us yet again, but ... I'm not going to do it. I'm not sorry you're stuck here with me. I would hate to do this one alone."

Landon's expression softened. "I'm not sorry I'm stuck here with you either. I didn't mean to snap at you." He pulled me forward and gave me a quick hug, pressing a kiss to my forehead before releasing me. "We'll get through this. We always do."

I offered a wan smile. "We always do."

"So, let's get moving." Landon extended his hand. "The lost city of Zeton awaits. Oh, and by the way, I know I've threatened it before but I'm totally going to kill Aunt Tillie when I get my hands on her."

"I'm so going to help you," Thistle growled. "That old lady won't know what's hit her when we get out of here. And, by the way, it's going to be my fist hitting her. She'd better start running now."

"HUH."

The door to Zeton was large and ridiculous. It looked like the door to a *Lord of the Rings* set, which was rather fitting because we were walking into a mountain. Er, well, kind of.

"Look at the walls." Marcus stood next to the archway and ran his fingers over what should've been rock. It wasn't rock, though. It was something else entirely. "It's ... well ... I think it's papier mâché. In fact, I think the entire mountain is made of papier mâché."

"Why would someone construct a mountain from papier mâché?" Landon challenged. "That seems like the worst material for construction like this."

"Soaps have limited budgets," Thistle volunteered. "The sets are never expensive ... or sometimes even believable. Practical sets, like hospitals and restaurants, look okay. Some of the others are less realistic."

"But papier mâché?" Landon shook his head. "Whatever. Let's find this diamond we're meant to claim and get the heck out of here. This place is creepy ... and weird." He narrowed his eyes as a woman with long red hair streamed past. She wore a lavender jumpsuit – something straight out of *Star Trek* – and the look she shot Marcus was nothing short of smoldering.

"Are you new?"

Marcus jolted at the question. "Um ... we're just checking out your setup to decide if we want to join the cause."

"Just out of curiosity, what is the cause?" I asked.

The woman turned a serene expression in my direction. "We're interested in pledging ourselves to the light and turning away from the darkness."

"That's a bit vague," Thistle noted. "What do you think that means?"

"It's probably a cult," I supplied. "Aunt Tillie doesn't know anything about real cults, so it's likely she cherry-picked whatever she saw on television and created some weird approximation of what she thinks a cult should be."

"That probably explains why there's an entire roomful of people over there doing what looks to be synchronized yoga," Clove said, pointing toward a large gymnasium. There had to be at least thirty people inside, all wearing matching jumpsuits – this time in blue. They were stretching and contorting their bodies as if driven by an unseen force.

"That's creepy, huh?"

Landon rubbed his hand over my back. "It is a little creepy. I doubt they're a dangerous cult, though."

"What makes you say that?"

"Well, look at their outfits." Landon flashed a charming grin that could still make me go weak in the knees at the appropriate moment. "Dangerous people don't wear spandex."

"Good point." I slipped my hand in Landon's and turned to survey the room. "One of the soaps had a story like this. I think it was *One Life to Live*."

"That's also the one that had the time travel, right?" Thistle asked. "I think I kind of remember that one."

"Time travel?" Landon didn't look as if he liked the sound of that. "Please tell me she's not going to force us to go through that again. I've had my fill of time travel."

"I think soaps offer her plenty of other ways to torture us," I replied. "I don't think we need to worry about time travel. Demonic possession and super villains are another story, though."

"Oh, I'm waiting for one of our stories to change so one of us is actually dating a brother or something," Thistle said. "That's a soap staple."

"Except we're not really related, so it won't be a big deal," Sam pointed out.

"No, but even hearing it suggested will be enough to kill the romance."

Landon shot me a pointed look. "If she even tries that I will lock her in her room for the rest of her life."

"She's going to outlive us all," Thistle muttered. "Plus, if you try, she'll do something worse than this."

"I'm not convinced there is anything worse than this," Landon argued. "Still, we're in an underground city that's supposed to be hidden, yet it has a billboard right next to it. I think we need to find our diamond and get out of here."

"I know you don't want to hear this, but I think it's going to be okay," I said. "If I remember correctly, this story ended well when I watched it with Aunt Tillie."

"Oh, yeah?" Landon cocked an eyebrow. "Did they ever explain how a city existed under a mountain and no one noticed it?"

"It's a soap. After a while you ignore the bigger-picture questions and just go with the flow."

"I'm not sure I can, but I'll give it a shot. In fact … ." Landon trailed off, shifting his eyes toward the center of the room.

I followed his gaze, my eyes widening when I recognized the familiar profile. "Is that ... ?"

"Dad?" Thistle made an odd face when she saw the man in question. In turn, the man who looked like Uncle Teddy flicked his eyes to us but didn't immediately speak. There was no recognition there, which made me realize we were dealing with an imaginary soap opera character that just happened to look like Thistle's father rather than the real deal. "What are you doing here?"

"Do I know you?" Teddy asked, his eyes busy. "Are you new to our brave new world?"

"Oh, geez." Thistle pinched the bridge of her nose. "Why doesn't it surprise me that Aunt Tillie made my dad a cult member?"

"Why does anything that woman does surprise you?" Landon challenged. "She's off her broom. I've known that since the moment I met her."

"And yet you still got shot for her," I reminded him. "Maybe you're just as crazy as she is."

"Why do you think we get along so well?" Landon teased, pressing a kiss to the tip of my nose.

"Oh, don't get all schmaltzy. We have no time for schmaltzy." Thistle warned, turning back to her father. "What's your name?"

"Flynn Warfield."

Thistle shook her head. "What do you do here, Flynn?"

"I'm second in command."

"Meaning?"

"Meaning I issue orders when our leader isn't available."

"That seems a little too on the nose," Landon said. "Still, he looks like Teddy for a reason. We might as well see if he can help us."

"I guess." Thistle tried again. "So ... um, Flynn ... do you know where we can find a diamond that's big enough to fuel a device that will freeze the world?" Thistle barely got out the question before she snorted. "There's something I never thought I'd hear myself say."

"We've all been there," Landon muttered.

"You're looking for a diamond?" The look on Teddy's face was hard to read.

"We are," Thistle confirmed. "We need it."

"I see." Teddy linked his fingers in front of him. "Why do you think we have diamonds here?"

"Because it says so on your sign."

"I don't believe that's true."

"Well, it is." Thistle's agitation was beginning to show. "I don't have time to mess around with you, Dad. I mean ... Flynn. Flynn is a stupid name, by the way. All I can hear playing through my head is 'in like Flynn,' and it makes me want to punch somebody."

"I recommend punching him," Clove suggested, pointing at Teddy.

"I'm not ruling it out."

Teddy watched with dispassionate eyes. "I don't believe we have what you need here. You'll have to look elsewhere."

"Well, we're not looking elsewhere," Thistle said. "We need a diamond. You're advertising them on your sign. That means you're going to give us a diamond."

Teddy's expression turned territorial. "And what makes you believe that?"

"Let's just call it a hunch."

"I can't help you." Teddy was firm. "The only diamond we have that size fuels our oxygenator. We'll die without it."

"Or you could just move to the surface and stop living like mole people," Landon suggested.

Teddy ignored the suggestion. "I can't help you."

"You have to help us," Thistle pressed. "We need that diamond, and ... you're not even real!"

Teddy balked. "What is that supposed to mean?"

"Forget it." Thistle waved off the question. "We need that diamond. Don't make us search for it."

"You can't have free rein over this facility," Teddy argued. "I won't allow it. In fact ... ." He snapped his head toward the gymnasium, where every occupant was now staring in our direction like a scene from the *Stepford Wives*. It was altogether eerie that they'd simply stopped doing their yoga poses and were now focused on us. "We will work together to thwart you."

"Thwart?" Landon shook his head. "Yeah, I should've seen this coming. You listen here, Teddy Flynn, we don't have time to mess around. We need that diamond and we're not going to stop until we get it."

"We can stop you." Teddy was firm. "Don't make us kill you."

The last sentence was uttered in a whisper, but it was one everyone in the gymnasium joined in saying together, so a creepy hiss wafted through the room, causing my blood to run cold.

"Oh, well, that's not freaky or anything," Landon said, sliding his arm around my waist.

"I already hate this place," Clove announced. "Screw the diamond. Let's get out of here."

I opened my mouth to agree, but was distracted when another figure hopped on the stage at the end of the room, his red jumpsuit standing out in a sea of pastels. The expression on the man's face was one of utter contempt.

"Oh, no," I muttered.

Landon followed my gaze. "Who is that? Do you recognize him?"

I shook my head. "No, but I sense something is about to happen."

"Why?"

"Because his jumpsuit is a different color and he's on a stage."

"Oh, well, go ahead and be logical."

The man on the stage raised his hand for everyone's attention. I spared a glance for Teddy and found his face had gone white.

"I am Flynn Warfield," the man announced.

"I thought you were Flynn Warfield," Thistle challenged her father.

"I ... um ... ." Teddy was at a loss for words.

"I am Flynn Warfield," the man at the front of the room repeated. "I was your second-in-command for twenty years until that man claimed to be me." He extended a knobby finger in Teddy's direction. "He said I was in an accident and needed reconstructive surgery. That was a lie!

"He locked me in a dungeon room in my own family's facility, but I escaped and am back," he continued. "I am the real Flynn Warfield, and I'm taking back my kingdom. All usurpers should beware. I'm not taking any prisoners."

"Oh, well, that sounds ominous." Landon turned so he could scan the room again. "Do you think they have a restaurant here? I'm starving."

∼

I was sad when your great-uncle died. I was lonely. Do you know what saved me? Knowing there were worse things out there … like evil twins, back-from-the-dead psychopaths and aliens that were allowed to hang out with little girls without being considered creepy. That's why soap operas rule.

– Aunt Tillie explaining the joys of soap operas

SIX

"I don't understand." Landon's pragmatic mind was having real trouble with a fake soap opera world. "How could one guy pretend to be the other guy and no one notice the difference?"

"You would be surprised how often that happens on soaps," I said. "A lot of times it happens because the original actor quit and they needed to recast. They often explain the change with an accident that required plastic surgery. Other times they simply ignore it.

"Then, when the original actor comes back, they do this sort of switch thing where they either pretend the facial reconstruction didn't happen or create a never-before-seen twin," I continued. "I think every soap has trotted this out a time or two."

"Max on *One Life to Live*," Clove volunteered.

"Todd on *One Life to Live*," Thistle added.

"It sounds like there's more than one life to live on that soap," Landon grumbled. "It looks like the red shirt is going to speak again. I can't wait to hear the rest of this."

"Zeton was built as a place for peace and happiness," Flynn continued. "That's what I envisioned when I set out to establish the community. I still believe in it, despite the fact that I was held in the basement for three years and no one noticed this imposter sullying my good name!"

He roared the final words as he pointed at Teddy. For his part, Thistle's father looked as if he'd rather be in a different hole in the ground.

"Does anyone else feel as if we're stuck in a high school Shakespeare production and the knives and poison are about to start flying?" Marcus asked.

Sadly, that felt like an apt comparison. "We need to get out of here."

"We need the diamond first," Landon argued. "We have to stick to the storyline. If it's one thing I've learned about Aunt Tillie's little magical lessons, if we don't stick to the storyline we'll be worse off."

"I'm not sure how it could get worse than this," Thistle noted, her eyes zeroing in on the rather impressive ... um, package ... on display thanks to the man standing next to her. Apparently underwear and boxer shorts were a no-no in Zeton, even though they desperately needed them thanks to the tight jumpsuits. "Seriously, it's like being trapped in a really weird porn movie."

"Hey!" Marcus snapped his fingers in front of Thistle's face to get her attention. "Don't look at that."

"Oh, it's not so funny now, is it?" Landon chortled. "When Bay's butt was getting pinched, everyone told me to suck it up. Now that Thistle has roaming eyes we need to get out of this mess. That's typical."

"I happened to believe we needed to get out of this mess before that," Marcus argued. "It's just ... hey, what is that guy doing?"

Marcus' attention moved back to the stage and, as with any good train wreck, I couldn't stop myself from looking. It seemed Flynn was in the middle of stripping out of his jumper ... and he had something clutched in his hand.

"I've decided to move Zeton to a fresh location, one that hasn't been corrupted by greed," Flynn announced. "The current location is a mess thanks to that man and his machinations. I'm not very happy with everyone else, either. I mean ... couldn't you have tested him with questions only I'd know the answers to?"

"We tried," a woman in the crowd replied. "He said he had amnesia."

"And you believed him?"

The woman shrugged. "He had a jumper. Where did he get the jumper if he wasn't you?"

"I believe you can find them at any cheap Halloween store," Clove offered helpfully.

"It doesn't matter," Flynn bellowed. "I am moving the location of Zeton. Only those I trust will be allowed to come with me."

"How do you expect to do that?" Teddy challenged, finding his voice. "You can't steal the heritage of this mountain, of this group, and co-opt it for a new group simply because you wish it. Zeton is much more than a place to live. If the people leave here, their immune systems will crash. They haven't been exposed to the outside world in decades."

"The door is right there," Landon offered. "It opens and closes pretty easily. I think they'll be fine."

"Silence," Teddy snapped. "You're the reason this is happening."

"Me?"

"You distracted me. You called me away when I should've been watching the prisoner."

"Hey, if you were the only one watching him for years on end, you have other issues." Landon's weariness came out to play. "Now, give me that diamond and we'll leave you to your domestic dispute."

"I will not." Teddy was firm. "You can torture me, make me listen to Barbra Streisand music and eat turnips, I still won't hand over the diamond."

"Oh, let's not get dramatic." Landon rolled his eyes. "I really hate this place."

"Besides, friend, that imposter is no longer in charge of the Diamond of Life," Flynn announced. "I am."

The crowd gasped as Flynn held up what looked to be a very cheap hunk of cut glass.

"You can't take that," Teddy shrieked. "You'll kill us if you do. The oxygenators won't work without the diamond."

"And yet we're breathing now," Landon pointed out. "In fact ... the door is literally right there. All you have to do is walk through it ... and stop at the nearest clothing store, because you'll get your ass beat on the street if you wear that. You'll be fine."

"It's not going to be fine," Teddy argued. "Zeton is falling."

"It is," Flynn agreed, clutching the diamond to his chest. "It will be reborn, though. I will see it reborn."

Landon lifted his hand in the air to get Flynn's attention, but it was already too late. The flamboyant man was opening a door set in the papier mâché rock, stopping only to cast a dramatic look at the room of panicking people. "I wish I could've saved you from this. Your undoing is on you."

And, with that, he disappeared through the door.

"Great," Landon spat. "Now we have to chase the freak with the diamond. I just know the next stop will be worse than this one ... if that's even possible."

Teddy, who was doing a good impersonation of a bad actor himself, clutched at his neck as he fell near Landon's feet. He clawed at his neck as if he was struggling for his very last breath. "Avenge us."

"The door is right there!" Landon barked. "You're not suffocating. It's all in your head."

"Come on." I grabbed Landon's arm and dragged him toward the stage. "You can't fix this. It's part of the story."

"But he's acting as if he's a fish out of water or something. It's ridiculous."

"This whole thing is ridiculous," Thistle said, leaving her father behind without a backward glance. "You might as well get used to it. We've got a long way to go before things get better. Aunt Tillie is barely getting started with us."

THE DOOR OPENED ON the docks.

I expected a dark hallway, maybe something resembling the planet

Hoth – without the snow, of course – but instead we found ourselves in a dimly lit harbor setting that made me want to check my shoes to make sure there wasn't a sea slug trying to climb my leg.

Landon was befuddled. "What the heck is this?"

"Docks," Clove answered. "See ... that's water and that's a boat."

The look Landon shot her was right out of the book Irritation 101. "Thank you, Clove. I never would've figured that out myself."

Clove merely shrugged. "You asked."

"Whatever," he mumbled under his breath before turning his attention to me. "What do you think?"

"I think we're here for a reason," I replied. "Aunt Tillie clearly wants us to see a lot of sets. At least we don't have to arrange for our own transportation. I wondered when we didn't see any cars on the road. You very rarely see vehicles on soaps ... unless it's for a scene in which someone is going to run someone else down."

"I guess we have that going for us." Landon tugged a restless hand through his hair. "What are we supposed to do here?"

I shrugged. "I don't know. I think the bigger question is: Where did Flynn go?"

"Yeah, that guy needs some Prozac," Thistle said.

"I think that's what happens when you're kept in a locked room for years," Marcus supplied. "You should think long and hard before trying to do that with Aunt Tillie. Do you want her ending up nuttier than she already is?"

Thistle's expression was appraising. "You usually stick up for Aunt Tillie no matter what. Things must be bad if you're turning on her."

"I'm not turning on her."

"She can't hear you. There's no reason to deny what you're feeling."

"I'm not turning on her." Marcus repeated the words, but the way he lifted his eyes to the sky made me think he believed Aunt Tillie was spying on us. I couldn't help but wonder about that, too. "I'm simply ... tired. We've been here only an hour, but it somehow feels longer."

"So much longer," Sam intoned. "I think this world is better than the fairy tale one, though. At least here I don't have to climb anyone's hair to save my beloved ... oh, and I don't have that pesky growing nose problem."

"Oh, I like when you call me that," Clove cooed, leaning closer to Sam and resting her cheek against his chest. "You're my beloved, too."

"Don't make me throw you in the water," Thistle snapped. "I can take only so much."

Clove scowled. "I wasn't talking to you."

"As long as I can hear you, you're talking to me."

"Knock it off, guys," I warned. "Now is not the time for a fight."

"When is the time for a fight?" Thistle challenged. "I would like to schedule it and set a warning on my phone so I don't forget."

Phone? Hmm. I dug in my pocket and came up empty. "Do you have your phone?"

Thistle balked. "Well ... no. It was a figure of speech."

"I'm not attacking you. I was simply asking."

"What does the phone have to do with anything?" Landon asked. "It's not as if we can call for help."

"I know. I think we know the way Aunt Tillie's mind works well enough to realize that we're all sleeping in our beds and not really here. I was simply curious."

"I have a phone," Sam announced, drawing out what looked to be an old Nokia from his pocket. "I haven't seen something like this in years."

Landon peered over his shoulder. "That's because they don't make them anymore."

"Why would Sam have a phone, but the rest of us don't?" Thistle asked. "He's Aunt Tillie's least favorite – which is saying something because we have Landon with us – and yet he gets a phone. I don't understand."

"Does it work?" Landon snagged the phone from Sam's hand, pressed some buttons and frowned. "It looks dead."

"I wouldn't count on that," Marcus said. "If she thought to include it, there's a reason."

"Yeah, I guess we'll find out eventually." Landon handed the phone back to Sam. "We need to find that Flynn guy. He's clearly our focus until something else pops up. He has the diamond we need ... or at least we think we need ... so we have to figure out where he would go next."

"I think I can help you with that."

The sultry voice from the shadows caught me off guard. I thought we were alone, just the six of us on ridiculously fake docks, but it seemed I was wrong. "Who's there?"

Landon instinctively stepped in front of me, pushing his arm out to keep Thistle and me behind him. He cast a pointed look at Sam to make sure he did the same with Clove. It was a fake world, so the odds of us really being hurt were slim, but that didn't mean Landon was taking any chances.

"Can I help you?"

The woman who stepped from the murk into the light was breathtaking. She was taller than me by a good three inches and she had long blond hair to her waist. Speaking of her waist, it was ridiculously small, even though her boobs could've claimed their own ZIP code.

"Hello, lover," she purred as she sauntered closer to Landon.

I knew it wasn't the time, yet I couldn't stop myself from growing territorial. "Hey!"

"Oh, finally I get a reaction out of you," Landon drawled, casting a quick look over his shoulder, his eyes gleaming when they locked with mine. "Now you care."

"If she pinches your butt I'm throwing her into the water," I warned.

"Duly noted." Landon lowered his arm, although he made sure to stand in front of the pack. The woman didn't look dangerous – unbelievably slutty, but not dangerous – so he clearly didn't feel the need to go all Terminator when it came to protection mode. "Do I know you?"

The woman's laugh was light and silky. "Is that supposed to be a joke?"

"Of course not. Um ... ." Landon looked to me for help.

"I'm Bay Winchester," I announced, extending my hand as I stepped forward.

"I'm Eden Rose." The woman's gaze was keen as she looked me up and down. "You look familiar, although I don't believe I've ever heard that name before."

"I think you're supposed to use your other name," Clove suggested.

"That name is ridiculous. I'm not using that name."

"Yes, because Eden Rose isn't a ridiculous name," Thistle muttered. "She does look really familiar. Do we know her from somewhere?"

"Are you talking about me?" Eden arched an eyebrow as she stared down Thistle. "I'm a lieutenant with the Camelot Falls Police Department."

"Oh, I must know her from work," Landon mused.

"If you worked with someone who looked like that in real life I'd cuff you to me and never let you leave the house again," I supplied.

Landon smirked. "Ah, it's not so funny when the curse is on the other foot, is it?"

"It's not funny at all." I looked Eden up and down with overt disgust. "Those can't possibly be real, by the way."

"Oh, they're real." Eden's expression was dismissive. "I've been waiting for you for more than an hour, Jericho. You were supposed to be here to give an update on the Michael Ferrigno case right after sunset. What took you so long?"

If Landon was bothered by her tone he didn't show it. "I had to go to an underground city and watch a bunch of freaks fake dying."

"You were there?" Eden was grave. "The loss of life at Zeton was enormous."

"Really? I'm sure if you wander over there you can just drag them outside and they'll make miraculous recoveries."

"That's not part of the mission." Eden was firm. "What do you have? Do you have the information we need to bring down Ferrigno?"

"Um ... no." Landon shook his head. "I'm working on it, though. I hope to have the information shortly."

"You have to work faster."

"I'm working as fast as I can."

"It's not fast enough." Eden adopted a pouty expression as she sidled closer. "I miss you, lover. I cry myself to sleep every night that you're not next to me."

"Oh, my ... Goddess." I thought my head might implode. "She's your girlfriend!"

"She's not my girlfriend," Landon protested.

"That's right," Eden confirmed. "We live together. We're supposed to be getting married in a few months. We're going to live happily ever after. I'm his fiancée."

My stomach twisted. "Yeah, because that makes it better."

"Hey, you're married," Landon reminded me. "Why wouldn't I have a girlfriend in this ... cesspool?"

"Because you're supposed to be in love with me."

"This is a fake world!" Landon exploded, his temper getting the better of him. "I can't control how Aunt Tillie wrote it. It's not as if I've really been cheating on you."

"What is going on here?" Eden planted her hands on her hips as her eyes bounced between us. "Is there something you want to tell me, Jericho?"

Landon nodded without hesitation. "Yes. Jericho is a stupid name."

"And?"

"And ... um ... I think we should stop seeing each other." Landon was clearly trying to appease me, but Eden didn't take it well. Instead she slapped him hard across the face, causing him to reel back. He wasn't even minimally recovered when she attacked a second time and threw a drink at him, the liquid splashing across his handsome features. "Hey!"

"Where did she get the drink?" Clove asked. "Did anyone see her carrying a drink?"

Thistle shook her head. "No, but throwing drinks is a soap staple. It doesn't really surprise me."

Eden moved to slap Landon again, but he caught her wrist before she could.

"Don't do that," Landon warned.

"Hey, my phone is ringing." Sam lost interest in the scene playing out in front of us and dug for his phone. "Should I answer it?"

Marcus nodded. "It's probably part of the story."

"Okay." Sam pressed the phone to his ear. "Hello?"

"You can't leave me," Eden screeched. "We're destined to be together. I will kill anyone who tries to get between us."

"Yeah, that sounds healthy," Landon deadpanned. "I really don't care. I think we need to take a break."

"Oh, of course you do," Eden sneered. "I know you've been running around behind my back. I assumed you were doing it because you had no choice, you had to or risk being found out and ultimately killed for your betrayal of Ferrigno. I guess I know better now, don't I?"

"I guess you do." Landon was blasé ... right up to the point when Eden wrenched her wrist free and grabbed the front of his shirt. With an ease that shouldn't have been possible given my knowledge of fabric and seams, she ripped Landon's shirt from his chest, leaving behind only two sleeves and a baffled look on his face. "What the ... ?"

"This is your doing," Eden hissed, rubbing the remnants of the shirt over her face as her eyes turned crazy and dangerous. "You'll rue the day you broke my heart!"

Landon was over the drama. "Give me back my shirt."

"No!" Eden continued rubbing it against her cheek. "It's all I have to remember you by. I won't forget any of this. You've broken me, wrecked me. You set off a bomb in my heart and now that it has exploded there are too many pieces to pick up."

"But ... ."

Landon didn't get a chance to finish his statement, because Sam had finished his phone call and he looked altogether sick to his stomach.

"What is it?" Clove asked, worried.

"I'm needed at the hospital," Sam replied woodenly. "I'm supposed to perform emergency brain surgery."

"Oh, well, that explains the phone." Thistle was clearly amused. "This world is starting to look up. I can't wait to see the hospital."

I want to be a fashion model, astronaut, writer, makeup company CEO and doctor on the weekends. That woman did it all in less than a year. At least she's never bored.
– Aunt Tillie picking a soap career

SEVEN

Eden was beyond conversation and her need to rub Landon's shirt over her face and chest was downright disturbing. Landon finally gave up trying to reclaim his clothing – it was beyond repair anyway – and focused on our next issue.

"I'm not doing it," Sam announced. "I don't care what you think, what you expect or how much you beg … it's simply not going to happen."

"We still have to go to the hospital," Landon said, folding his arms over his chest as he attempted to cover his bare skin. He was clearly uncomfortable. "You wouldn't have gotten the call unless we were supposed to go there next."

"Yes, but I'm a brain surgeon on weekends," Sam said. "That's what that clip show thing said. They called me for brain surgery. There's no way I'm doing that."

"I doubt very much you're going to have to do it," I supplied. "It's a soap opera, not a medical show. They never show the nitty-gritty on a soap opera. At most they'll show a couple close-ups of your face. There's no way anyone is going to put a scalpel in your hand."

Sam wasn't convinced. "I'm not doing it."

Landon held up his hands to stave off an argument. "You're not going to have to perform surgery. I can virtually guarantee that. We still need to head to the hospital."

Sam wasn't about to be placated. "I'm not doing surgery."

"And I'm sick of hearing you say that." Landon put a hand to my elbow to direct me toward the opposite end of the dock. "Let's get going."

"How do you know that's the right direction?"

"Because the only thing in that direction is Zeton and I have no intention of going back there."

"Fair enough." I fell into step with him, refusing to look over my shoulder to make sure everyone else followed. I figured they were on their own if they chose to separate. The only one I was determined to stay close to was Landon. I'd never been lost in one of Aunt Tillie's worlds without him – at least not for an extended period – and I wasn't about to start now.

"Do you want to tell me what you're thinking?" Landon's voice was soft.

"I'm not sure what I'm thinking. It's a lot to process."

"Yeah, that's not going to work on me."

"Well, for starters, I think it's funny that you're covering your chest that way. It's not as if anyone is staring at your nipples or anything."

Landon made a derisive snort in the back of his throat. "I feel exposed."

"We're not really on television. You're okay."

Landon reluctantly dropped his arms, although he didn't look thrilled with his decision. "I'm starting to think Aunt Tillie is crazy because she watches soap operas. When I first met her I thought she was confused because of old age. After knowing her a bit I assumed it was because she simply liked being crazy. Now I think it's the soap operas making her wonky. I'm going to ban her from watching them if we ever get out of here."

It was a somber moment, but I couldn't stop myself from laughing. "She's not crazy. She only wants people to think she's crazy. She's smarter than almost everyone I know."

"Is that saying much?"

"I was including you in the group."

"Ha, ha." Landon poked my side. "You haven't said much about what just happened. Are you still ... upset?"

"Upset?" I cocked an eyebrow. "I don't know if 'upset' is the word. I was surprised more than anything else."

Landon snorted. "Bay, if you were a cat you would've started hissing when you saw her. Your back would've arched and you would've made that snarling sound cats make while preparing themselves to claw their enemies to death."

"I think you're exaggerating."

"And I think it was kind of funny."

"You didn't think it was funny when Michael pinched my butt."

"Because that was weird."

"And that woman rolling around on the dock and rubbing her face against your shirt as if she's a dog and memorizing your scent, that's normal?"

"Well, when you phrase it like that ... ." Landon's smile was sheepish when he spared me a look. "Bay, you can't let this stuff get to you. I know it's hypocritical for me to say given how I reacted with the happy butt pincher, but it's true. Aunt Tillie wants us to overreact. We need to remain calm."

"That's easier said than done." I glanced over my shoulder and found Clove and Sam trailing us, Clove's hand on her boyfriend's arm as she attempted to soothe him. I adjusted my tone. "We'd better hope he's not really expected to perform surgery."

"I was just thinking the same thing."

"**NO!**"

Sam was beside himself when the hospital's chief of staff, who just happened to look a lot like Clove's father Warren, met us at the front door of the facility.

"We don't have much time." Warren grabbed Sam's arm and tugged him forward. "We need you. We need your gift."

"Absolutely not!" Sam's eyes were wild with fear. "I refuse."

"You must." Warren didn't back down. "The man's life is in danger. He won't last long. He's already overcome so much."

"I don't really care if he's overcome a pack of zombies," Sam fired back. "I'm not doing it."

"You don't understand," Warren pressed. "It's Flynn Warfield. He's a celebrity in the field of metaphysical belief systems."

Landon and I exchanged a weighted look. Landon cleared his throat to get Warren's attention. "Flynn Warfield?"

Warren nodded. "Then you've heard of him?"

"A little something here and there," Landon replied. "I have no idea what a metaphysical belief system is, but I've heard of Flynn." He shifted his eyes to Sam. "I believe you have to do the surgery."

Sam's expression was murderous. "No means no!"

"Oh, you're such a kidder." Warren gave Sam's shoulder a good squeeze. "You're the best weekend brain surgeon that we have. This man will die without you."

"That's kind of exciting." Clove's eyes sparkled. "I always wondered what it would be like to date a doctor."

If looks could kill, Sam would've struck his beloved dead with a single glare. "You're on my list, Clove," he announced. "You're right at the top. You're even beating out Aunt Tillie right now."

"That's a little sad," Thistle noted. "I guess you're even more of a kvetch than we realized, huh?"

"I'll make you eat soap opera dirt if you're not careful," Clove shot back. "I bet it's even grosser than real dirt. That's how Aunt Tillie does things."

Thistle apparently thought the threat had weight, because she wisely shut her mouth. That didn't mean I could.

"I think you have to do the surgery, Sam," I prodded. "We need that diamond, and if Flynn is in surgery … ."

Sam realized what I was getting at … and he apparently didn't like it. "You want me to try to steal a diamond from him while I'm conducting surgery?"

"Do you have a better idea?"

Sam's mouth moved, but no sound came out. It was almost as if he was talking silently to himself. Finally, he regrouped enough to utter a sentence. "You just took Clove's spot on top of my list."

"Yay!" Clove clapped her hands. "I didn't like being at the top of your list. This is so much better."

"Yeah, yeah." Sam rolled his eyes, cringing when he realized Warren was watching him. "Why are you still here?"

"I'm waiting for you." Warren wasn't letting up. Sam seemed to finally realize that, because he looked resigned. "We need to get moving now."

"Fine." Sam scratched at an invisible itch on the side of his nose. "I'll do brain surgery. That seems to be the only way out of this. So, I will do it. I'll be a brain surgeon on weekends."

"You're so strong, honey." Clove patted his arm. "I've never been more proud of you than I am right now."

"That doesn't make me feel better, Clove," Sam snapped.

"We'll need you, too, Cinder," Warren added, turning to Clove.

"Me?" Clove's features turned white. "Why would you need me?"

"You're a weekend nurse."

"But ... ." Clove looked panicked. "I can't be a nurse. I most certainly can't sit through surgery. You know how I feel about blood."

"This must be one of the other personalities talking," Warren noted. "That's okay. We thought ahead for when this happened. Each personality passed the nursing exam, so you're good to go."

"What?" Clove was flabbergasted. "No way. Uh-uh. Not gonna happen."

"Oh, now it's a big deal," Sam intoned. "It wasn't a big deal when it was me. Now that it's you, though ... ."

"I thought Clove was a naughty nurse," Thistle argued. "That's not like a real nurse. It's more like on Halloween when I was a naughty stewardess and I helped Marcus stow his luggage in the overhead compartment."

"Don't be gross," Landon barked, pressing his eyes shut.

"I concur." Warren's smile never wavered as he focused on Clove. "We need both of you to save a man's life. You can't turn your back on something like that, can you?"

Clove was morose. "I guess not." She darted a hateful look in my direction. "I'm not sure how yet, but I'm almost positive this is your fault. Thistle's, too. When this is over, I'm going to make you both eat so much dirt you'll choke to death."

For lack of anything better to do, I offered up a sarcastic salute. "Good luck. May fortune favor the foolish ... and brave."

Clove narrowed her eyes to dangerous slits. "You're dead to me."

LANDON FOUND A SHIRT in the lost-and-found box. It featured a cat with a pretty pink bow. I had to bite the inside of my cheek to keep from laughing when I saw it.

"Don't say a word," Landon warned, turning his attention to Thistle and Marcus. "Have you heard anything on the surgery?"

"They've been gone like twenty minutes," Marcus replied. "You can't perform brain surgery in twenty minutes."

"It's a soap," Thistle reminded him. "You can do anything in twenty minutes on a soap."

"Including being a brain surgeon on weekends. I ... ." I had no idea what I was going to say. I'm sure it would've been pithy and bright, though. I lost my train of thought when I saw the woman in the nurse's uniform crossing to us. She had a certain edge that wouldn't let me look away.

Much like Eden, she was tall, thin and busty. I knew before she opened her mouth that she was coming for Landon. Her flirty gaze and swishing hips were distinct clues.

"Jericho." She didn't acknowledge the rest of us before sliding her hand into Landon's hair and pressing her mouth to his.

To his credit, Landon immediately pushed her back. "What are you doing?" he sputtered.

"I've been waiting for your call for a week," the nurse said, her bottom lip jutting into the perfect pout. "You were supposed to call me. This is not how you treat the woman you're going to propose to once you're done working undercover."

"Ooh, soap Landon is a total tool," Thistle supplied, smirking. "I should've seen that coming."

"Jericho is a tool," Landon corrected, doing his best to keep the nurse from stroking her hands over his chest. "Jericho is not me."

"Of course you're Jericho," the nurse countered. "We've been together for a year."

"Yeah, well … ." Landon licked his lips and looked at me. "Do you want to help?"

"Far be it from me to get between you and your fiancée."

"Knock it off. This isn't my fault."

"No, but it's still irritating."

"Fine." Landon's eyes fired as he turned back to his randy nurse. "Listen … um … what is your name?"

"You don't know my name?" The nurse was incensed.

"He has a head injury," Marcus offered helpfully. "He has partial amnesia."

Landon made a growling sound. "Like she's going to believe that."

"It's a soap."

"You have amnesia?" The nurse's voice turned soft. "My poor baby!" She grabbed Landon's head and pressed it to her ample breasts. "I'll take care of you. I'll make you remember me if it's the last thing I do. We'll fall in love all over again."

"Oh, geez." Landon struggled to pull away, although he didn't quite manage it. Part of me couldn't help but wonder if he was putting his full strength behind the effort.

"My name is Summer Glade," the nurse announced. "We've been in love since the moment we locked eyes across a smoky bar."

"A lovely story," Thistle said. "Just out of curiosity, did you sleep together the first night you met?"

"Of course." Summer's expression didn't shift. "I told you, it was love at first sight. We even got a great song for the big montage at the end. I just can't remember the name of it. I believe it was by Nickelback."

Landon groaned. "What does she mean about the song?"

"On a soap you always get a song for sex," I explained, my tone icy as I glared. Landon's head was still pressed against Summer's chest and he'd ceased struggling. "It's like a montage. By the way, are you trying to see if you can hear the ocean in those things?"

"What?" Landon furrowed his brow. "Oh." He gathered his strength for a final push and jerked away, raising a hand when Summer reached for him a second time. "Don't! I have amnesia. You're making me uncomfortable."

"I bet you're glad I gave you that story, huh?" Marcus winked as Landon scowled. "I'm starting to get this world."

"And Landon still isn't," Thistle said. "It's kind of funny."

"You're all on my list," Landon said. "I won't forget this."

"I thought you forgot everything," Summer challenged. "Isn't that why you don't remember me?"

"Do you know what I don't get," I offered. "Why do you have fiancées all over this place? Who has more than one fiancée?"

"We're not engaged yet," Summer corrected. "He's going to propose once his undercover assignment is completed."

"I must not be very good at the undercover thing if everyone knows what I'm doing," Landon noted.

"No, honey bunny, you're the best." Summer grasped at Landon's head again, but he smoothly sidestepped her.

"Knock that off!" Landon extended a warning finger. "I'm not your honey bunny. I'll never be your honey bunny."

"Excuse me?" Summer turned shrill as she planted her hands on her hips. "If you're not my honey bunny, whose honey bunny are you?"

Landon jerked a thumb in my direction. I totally should've seen that coming, by the way. "I'm her honey bunny. Er, well, she's my sweetie. It doesn't really matter. I'm not going to marry you."

"Oh, really." Summer narrowed her eyes until they were nothing but glittering strips of hatred. "Are you breaking up with me?"

"I guess I am."

"Well then." Summer took two deliberate steps forward, grabbed the front of Landon's shirt before he could slap away her hands, and tugged as hard as she could. The shirt, which should've held together better, ripped down the center, and Summer gripped the tattered remains in her fist as she began to vibrate with anger. "You'll be sorry you did this! I'll make you sorry."

Landon, his face awash with disbelief, stared down at his bare chest. "Again? How did this happen again?"

Thistle was laughing so hard she bent at the waist, resting her hands on top of her knees. "Oh, this is freaking priceless!"

"Why aren't women throwing themselves at me?" Marcus complained. "I look more like a soap star than he does."

Thistle sobered. "Are you honestly complaining about that?"

"It's not that I want another girlfriend," Marcus stressed. "It's just ... I'm better looking than him. You believe that, right?"

"Oh, I'm not answering that." Thistle turned to me. "This world is kind of funny at times. I'm starting to like it."

"That makes one of us," I said. "We need to find Sam and Clove to see if they have the diamond. In fact ... ." I trailed off when I saw Clove darting in our direction. She looked paler than normal – even more ashen than when she realized she would have to sit in and participate with brain surgery – and she made a beeline straight for us. "What's wrong?"

Landon straightened his shoulders and swiveled. "Did something happen?"

Clove remained focused on me. "You have to come. We have a situation."

"I'll say we have a situation," Thistle said. "Landon apparently has girlfriends stashed everywhere, and all of them are batshit crazy."

"Bay's not crazy," Landon shot back.

"Oh, you're driving me there," I said. "What's wrong, Clove?"

"Sam is in trouble." Clove was grim. "We lost Flynn on the operating table – and wait until I tell you about that situation – and now he's been called in front of the board for disciplinary action."

"So? Tell him to get out of it," Landon ordered. "We don't have time for that."

"He can't. Guards took him away."

"In a hospital?" That made absolutely no sense. "What do you want us to do?"

"They want to see all of us, too. They're waiting for us."

It seemed our story had taken another turn. I heaved a sigh. "Okay. I guess we know where we're going next."

"Let's just hope Landon doesn't have another girlfriend in there," Thistle said. "They seem to be getting crazier. The next one might very well be armed."

Now that was a sobering thought.

Only on soaps is it possible for a character to walk into a room looking like a blond god and come out with an entirely different face and a different hair color and have nobody comment on it. That's not even remotely believable … and I want realism when I'm watching a guy figure out that his father had a woman locked in a secret mansion room for twenty years.

– Winnie on the plausibility of soap operas

EIGHT

Landon grabbed another shirt from the lost-and-found box. This one featured a smiling cow wearing a tiara. While I found Landon's new shirt adorable, one look at him told me he felt the opposite. Apparently Aunt Tillie's sense of humor was an acquired taste.

"Why would they call a medical board hearing right after a death?" Landon asked as we followed Clove down the hallway behind the nurse's station. "Usually these things need an investigation and sworn statements first."

"It's a soap."

"That seems to be your excuse for everything."

"I don't know what you want me to say!" I snapped out the words with more vitriol than I intended. The look on Landon's face told me he didn't appreciate my tone. "I'm sorry. I didn't mean to be so ... mean."

Landon ran his tongue over his teeth, debating. "Sweetie, you can't let this get to you. That's what she wants. I know it's easier said than done, but this is all her being ... well, her."

"I didn't mean to snap at you. It's not your fault every woman in this world goes crazy and rips your shirt off."

"Yeah, what's that about?"

I shrugged. "Just Aunt Tillie's sense of humor rearing its conical hat ... and then laughing at us from afar."

"Well, it's getting old ... and fast."

"Yeah."

Clove seemed to know where to go, so we followed without complaint. When we walked into a wide conference room with a rectangular table in the center, I knew things were about to get interesting.

Three people – three women, in fact – sat behind the table. All of them wore doctor's coats and looked stern as they stared at Sam. For his part, Sam's color was back, but he looked oddly uncomfortable as he sat in a chair in the middle of the room.

"What's going on?" I asked, my eyes drifting to the doctors. "Why are Mom, Marnie and Twila here?"

"I don't think it's really them," Sam replied. "They keep asking me about being a brain surgeon on weekends and whether it's fulfilling. They're also interested in free legal advice, because it seems Winnie is a beauty company executive on the side and she's looking to incorporate."

"And I'm a ventriloquist," Twila added.

"Oh, well, that seems to fit," I muttered.

"I'm also a mime." As if to demonstrate, Twila started moving her hands while she pretended to be trapped in an invisible box.

"Very authentic," Thistle noted. "What are we doing here?"

"We're here to see if Dr. Wharton will be allowed to keep his medical license," Marnie said gravely. "He made several errors in surgery and a man died. We can't simply overlook that."

"Oh, well, that makes sense." I shook my head. "I'm sure Sam – I mean Dr. Wharton – is willing to give up his medical license if it means he can get out of here." I looked to Sam for confirmation. "Right?"

Sam nodded vigorously. "Absolutely!"

"Now, don't be hasty," Clove countered. "I've always wanted to have sex with a doctor."

"He's not really a doctor," I pointed out.

"Close enough."

"I'm starting to feel unloved, Clove," Sam snapped. "I thought you were happy with our life together."

Clove balked. "I am. It's just ... haven't you ever had a certain fantasy? I want to play doctor before we leave. Sue me."

"Fine. Then you have to dress up like a naughty nurse."

"Done."

Apparently Sam wasn't expecting Clove to capitulate so easily, because his eyebrows practically flew up his forehead. "Okay. Well ... um ... what were we talking about again?" He flicked his eyes to the table and found Winnie, Marnie and Twila glaring at him. "Why does this feel so familiar?"

"Because Aunt Tillie enjoys having fun at our expense," Landon replied. "As for this ... meeting ... we need to get through it. I guarantee we won't find that diamond in this room."

"I can mime being a diamond," Twila offered. "I'm really good at it."

Landon opened his mouth to comment, but snapped his mouth shut, instead flashing an enthusiastic thumbs-up to Twila.

"Let's just get this over with," I suggested. "What does Dr. Wharton need to do to keep his medical license?"

"He needs to tell us exactly what happened in that surgery," Mom replied. "Then we'll vote on the outcome. That's it."

"That sounds easy," Sam said, exhaling heavily.

Yeah, it sounded a little too easy. "Dr. Wharton isn't going to face any other repercussions besides losing his medical license if he's found guilty, right?"

Landon slid me a sidelong look. "Why did you ask that?"

I lifted a finger to still him. "Just wait."

"Of course not," Mom scoffed. "We handle his medical license. She handles the rest of it." Mom jerked her thumb to the door over her shoulder, which opened to allow Eden entrance. Thankfully she wasn't rubbing Landon's shirt against her face any longer, but that didn't make her look any saner. "Eden will decide if Dr. Wharton is being brought up on criminal charges."

"Of course she will." I looked to Landon. "This one is on you, big guy."

"You're going to owe me an entire weekend of naked bacon wrestling when this is over," Landon grumbled, taking a step forward. "I'm going to make you sign a contract and everything."

"Do I even want to know what naked bacon wrestling is?" Thistle asked.

"I'm kind of intrigued," Marcus said.

"I'm grossed out," Clove added.

"We're not talking about this," I argued. "Focus on the problem in front of us. We need to keep Sam out of ... whatever crazy web that nutbag is going to weave."

"I have no idea what you're talking about." Eden adopted an innocent façade. "I'm simply here to do my job. I'm a diligent employee. Jericho knows that better than anyone."

"You're up, Jericho," I prodded, bowing a bit as I held out my hand.

Landon ignored my tone and forced a smile. "It's good to see you, Eden. I've been worried about you after our ... breakup."

"Oh, don't play coy with me," Eden hissed as she strode forward, not stopping until she was directly in front of Landon. "I know what kind of game you're playing."

"I simply want to make sure that an innocent doctor isn't punished for something that wasn't his fault."

"Why? What's in it for you?"

"Nothing."

"What's in it for her?" Eden inclined her chin toward me. "I know you're only doing this to protect her."

I thought Landon might argue – he had that sort of look on his face – but instead he changed tactics. "I'm not trying to protect her," Landon whispered. I could hear him, but just barely. "I'm undercover and I have to use her for information. I can't talk about this in front of her."

Eden's eyes widened. "But you said ... ."

"I have to maintain cover in front of her at all costs. The fate of the entire investigation rests on it."

I did my best to maintain a neutral expression, but it wasn't easy.

"So you're still in love with me?" Eden asked hopefully.

"I'm ... very fond of you and hopeful you'll do the right thing," Landon gritted out, being careful not to make eye contact with me. I think he was afraid what he would find, but I knew he was simply doing his best to speed things along.

Eden studied Landon's face for what felt like forever. Finally, she offered a curt nod and turned to Mom, Winnie and Twila. "I've heard enough. There will be no criminal charges filed against Dr. Wharton."

Thistle leaned closer to me. "We didn't present any evidence."

"Who cares? This has already gone on far too long."

"Yeah, we're in a boring part," Thistle agreed. "In fact ... ."

When she didn't finish her sentence, I turned to face her and found her eyes glued toward a window near the ceiling. I followed her gaze, frowning when I realized we were looking at an observation room of sorts.

"Why would that be there?" I asked, confused. "This isn't an operating room."

"No, but look who's standing at the far end down there."

I gasped when I saw Aunt Tillie prancing in front of the window. She wore a loud evening gown with a peacock pattern, and one of those ostentatious hats with netting that covered her right eye. She waved with her right hand and held up the fake-looking diamond with her left.

"Son of a ... !"

"What?" Landon turned in that direction, swearing under his breath when he saw her. "I guess we know where the diamond is."

Aunt Tillie waited until she was sure everyone saw her before turning on her heel and disappearing.

"We have to chase her," Marcus said. "We need that diamond. That's why she has it."

"I know." Landon made a growling sound in the back of his throat. "She's officially on my last nerve."

"Welcome to my world," Thistle said. "It sucks sometimes."

THE HOSPITAL WAS A virtual maze. We did our best to follow Aunt Tillie, even though we kept losing sight of her. When that happened, she let loose a creepy giggle that allowed us to give chase. By the fifth time it happened, we were flustered, and annoyance threatened to overtake our group.

"I'm going to rip her throat out if she doesn't stop making that noise," Thistle groused. "I'm not joking. Between that and the music, it's too much."

"The music is for our montage," I pointed out. "If we were actually on a soap right now the music would be part of the chase."

"Yeah, what is it with the montages?" Landon asked. "You were going to explain it earlier, but then we got distracted."

"I'm still distracted," Thistle volunteered. "Your T-shirt is the most distracting thing I've ever seen."

Landon pretended he didn't hear her. "The music montages, Bay."

"It's a normal thing on soaps. I don't know why."

"Well, it's weird." Landon leaned against a wall and rubbed his forehead. "Does anyone else feel as if we've been going in circles for hours?"

"Why do you think she used a montage?" I asked. "She wants us to feel as if it's been hours. Real time is closer to ten minutes, but I'm exhausted from all the walking we've been doing."

"I'm more tired of the song and the giggling," Thistle said. "I'm also beyond agitated with the fact that we're still stuck in this world. How long are we supposed to put up with this?"

"Until she's finished punishing us."

"You're going to blame me for this, aren't you?" Thistle's voice was laced with challenge.

I shrugged. "Technically it's both our fault. I let you talk me into cursing her."

"And now we're all paying the price," Clove supplied, earning a dark look from Thistle. "What? I'm innocent in all of this. You guys got me in trouble. It doesn't seem fair."

"Yeah, yeah." Thistle waved off the complaint. "We need to get ahead of her. I don't like being behind."

"How are we possibly going to figure out what she has planned?" I challenged. "She's obviously given this place a lot of thought. I mean ... look at that guy." I pointed toward a handsome doctor as he walked into the room directly in front of us. "We've passed him three times now."

"Why is that important?" Landon asked, genuinely curious. "Does he play into this?"

"I don't think so, but I made note because he's going to look different when he comes out of that room. We've passed him three times and each time it happens. Watch."

As if on cue, the door opened to allow a different man to exit. He wore the same lab coat, shoes and blue stethoscope as the first.

"What was that?" Landon straightened his back. "Is that supposed to be the same guy?"

I nodded. "Two weeks ago I was talking to Aunt Tillie while she watched *General Hospital*. She was complaining because one of her favorite characters was recast. They didn't even announce it. He went to bed one night with one actor playing him and woke the next morning with a different actor playing him. Aunt Tillie was all worked up because she thought the woman who played his love interest on the show should've noticed they were two different men."

"She's watched soaps long enough to know that's normal," Thistle pointed out. "Abrupt recasts happen all the time."

"And no one thinks that's weird?" Landon shook his head. "I don't get it. There's no logic in this world."

"Yes, because the fairy tale world was an education on strict logic," Sam said.

I swallowed a chuckle as Landon scorched him with a dark look. "I don't think the recast thing is important in the grand scheme of things. It's just an added detail I picked up. I think Aunt Tillie has been plotting this world for a long time. There's no way she came up with this in a night, especially on a night we were drinking."

"So you think she was going to shove us here no matter what," Clove surmised. "She only did it last night because she was agitated."

I nodded. "I think we were always going to end up here eventually."

"I just want to know how many of these worlds she has planned for us," Landon said. "She watches a lot of television. I'm guessing she enjoys doing this crap enough that she's going to shove us in a *Star Trek* episode at some point just to get a few laughs."

"I'm less worried about *Star Trek* than I am about her affinity for *Game of Thrones* and *The Walking Dead*."

Landon chuckled. "Every once in a while you show flashes of being an optimist. I don't know why, but it makes me laugh."

"I don't know why either." I leaned my head against his shoulder, smiling as he pressed a kiss to my forehead. "We have to find her. We won't get out of here until we do."

"So I guess we should get moving, huh?" Landon slid his arm around my back, furrowing his brow when he focused on the room across the hallway. The window was open, so we could see inside. "One minute ago there was a kid in that bed. Now there's a teenager."

I turned in that direction, pursing my lips. "Does the kid look sick?"

"They were fussing over the smaller kid's head, and he had a big bandage on it," Landon replied. "From what I could tell, he didn't have an injury."

"That's not unheard of. It's not as if they shave people's heads when they're hurt on soaps. They just pretend they manage to conduct surgery without ruining anyone's hairline."

"That's stupid."

"You seem to be saying that a lot today."

"I have a feeling I'm going to keep saying it, too," Landon said. "The thing is ... now there's a teenager in that bed. He's wearing the same bandage – although it's not even like the last one – and the same set of parents are sitting watch. What's going on?"

"They age soap kids a lot," I explained. "Very few soap kids keep their roles for the duration. Soaps usually skip the unfortunate puberty stage. They hire cute kids and then replace them with hot teenagers."

"I see." Landon made a clucking sound with his tongue. "That's a bit ... extreme."

"It's a soap."

"I'm sure I'll get used to it eventually."

"Hopefully we won't be here that long." I pushed myself away from the wall. "We need to find Aunt Tillie."

"Yeah, but I think we lost her trail."

As if on cue, the giggling started again.

"I'm so going to bash that old lady's face in," Thistle muttered. "I'm going to enjoy doing it, too. I'm going to sit on her chest and poke it until she cries witch and tells the world I'm smarter and stronger than her."

"And I thought the people in the soap world were delusional," Landon drawled.

Thistle cocked an eyebrow. "You're on my list."

I heaved out a sigh. "I see we all have lists this go-around. It should be fun when we land back home."

If you could bring anyone back from the dead, who would it be? I've always thought that was over-used on soaps, but I get it now. I often wish I could kill people with the power of my mind and then regret thinking bad thoughts after the fact. If people could come back from the dead – and not in a creepy zombie way – then I could totally kill with impunity and no one would care.

– Aunt Tillie explaining why murder, at least in her case, isn't an issue

NINE

"Jericho?"

The face that cut us off in the hallway that led to the basement – which was where Aunt Tillie's infuriating laughter emanated from – belonged to a woman who couldn't be a day over twenty. Not only was she young and fresh-faced, she was thin and stacked. The latter part was illustrated to perfection thanks to her candy striper uniform. Wait ... are candy stripers even a thing anymore?

Landon pulled up short. "Do I know you?"

"Are you ... joking?"

"No. I have amnesia."

I marveled at how quickly Landon embraced the amnesia storyline. He whipped out the explanation whenever questioned at this point. The characters were predisposed to believe it, so I understood the inclination.

"You have amnesia?" The girl's face twisted into an expression that could only be described as heartbreaking. I didn't like her on sight, so it made me want to laugh. "But ... that will ruin everything." Her lower lip quivered as her eyes filled with tears. "Are you saying you don't remember me?"

"Oh, I can't take this." Landon scrubbed his hands over his cheeks. "She doesn't look old enough to play this part of the game."

"I'm nineteen," the girl huffed.

"Definitely not old enough." Landon flicked his eyes to me. "You know this isn't real, right?"

Even though the earlier girlfriends irritated me, I couldn't help feeling for him in this instance. She did look really young, and Landon wasn't the type to prey on vulnerable young women. "I know. I'm sorry. Aunt Tillie doesn't care how she has her fun ... as long as she has it."

"I don't understand how you can't remember me," the girl pressed. "It's me, Jericho. It's the love of your life ... Sandy Shores."

"Oh, Sandy Shores?" Thistle rolled her eyes as she barked out a laugh. "Aunt Tillie must've had a field day coming up with these names."

Sandy was offended. "What's wrong with my name?"

"I don't even know where to begin," Thistle replied. "When I can marvel at the stupidity of a name, though, you know something is wrong."

"I was named after my grandmother," Sandy announced. "She was a brilliant woman who served as the first female head of surgery at this very hospital."

"Oh, well, that's a nice legacy," I offered.

Sandy ignored me. "She conducted the first conscious brain transplant in history."

"A brain transplant, huh?" Landon didn't look impressed. "Well, that's something to be proud of, Sandy. I'm glad for your good memories about your grandmother. That's probably a good thing – a good role model – for you to emulate."

"Wait ... did you say conscious?" Marcus interjected. "Does that mean the patient was conscious during the surgery?"

"It does."

"See, that's not possible," Marcus complained.

"And a brain transplant when both parties are unconscious is possible?" Sam challenged. "I'm not a real brain surgeon, but even I know that's not possible."

"I think it would be neat," Clove said. "Imagine having your brain moved to someone else's body. I would want to be transported to Megan Fox's body. I called it. No one else can have her."

Even though I often found Clove's ideas amusing, this time I couldn't hide my disdain. "Then you'll have to sleep with her husband ... and she's already had three kids."

"I just want her body, not her kids."

"Oh, well, at least you've figured it out," I muttered.

"This is a stupid conversation," Sam complained.

"We've had way worse," Thistle pointed out. "Where have you been?"

Sam shot her a dark look. "You're really on my last nerve."

"Right back at you."

"This is getting us nowhere," I said, raising my hands to silence the others. "We need to find Aunt Tillie. She has the diamond and she's obviously leading us to a particular place. As much as I hate that giggling she's doing, I don't see where we have many options."

"I agree with Bay," Landon said, doing his best to ignore the looks Sandy kept lobbing at him. She was making a big show of widening her eyes to saucer-like proportions while allowing the occasional strategic tear to drop. "We need to get moving."

"But ... what about me?" Sandy challenged, putting her hand on Landon's arm to keep him from moving past her.

"I have a job to do," Landon said gently. "I'm sure we'll meet up later to talk about ... how you should be dating boys your own age."

"I don't want to date boys my own age."

"You'll get used to it."

"But ... I love you." Sandy's lower lip quivered to perfection. "There are times when I look at you while you're sleeping – I film you sometimes when you don't know it so I can re-watch the video when you're undercover and fill my heart with the love I so desperately miss while you're away – and I just know that our souls were meant to join."

"I think I just threw up in my mouth a little bit," Thistle drawled.

She wasn't the only one. "Sandy, I'm sure that your feelings for Jericho are ... something to behold," I started. "But we're on an undercover assignment. He can't get his memory back until we finish it."

Sandy's eyes were full of loathing when they locked with mine. "I know who you are."

"Okay."

"You're Michael Ferrigno's wife," Sandy continued. "Jericho is investigating him. He's going to bring him down. And, when he does, I'm going to get the love of my life back and you're going to get nothing."

"Okay, time out." Landon made a tee with his hands. "What kind of undercover police officer tells everyone about the case he's working on? That's not how it works. Did I tell you I was an undercover police officer when we met, Bay?"

I shook my head. "No, but you did hit on me while undercover."

"Barely."

"You still did it."

"Yeah, and look how that worked out," Landon pressed. "We're living together. We're happy – when crap like this doesn't pop up, I mean – and we're in love. I don't see where I did anything wrong during my first assignment."

"You definitely didn't do anything wrong," I agreed. "You even got shot saving me."

"Stop bringing that up," Landon ordered. "I know it makes you feel guilty, but I'm over it. I don't like hearing about it."

"You were shot?" Sandy's face twisted with anger. "Is that how you got amnesia?"

"What? Oh, sure." Landon absently ran his hand through his hair. "We need to get moving. I want to find Aunt Tillie and that stupid diamond. This world gets stranger by the minute and I'm not sure I can take much more of it."

"So you're just leaving?" Sandy's voice rose. "How can you walk away given everything we've meant to each other?"

"I've merely given it some thought." Landon adopted a pragmatic tone. "I want to do the right thing by you. That means letting you go. Sometimes if you really, really ... feel uncomfortable with a situation ... it's best to let the other person go so he or she can find true love."

Sandy's expression was hard to read. "And that's what you want? To let me go?"

Landon nodded. "I'm sorry."

"No, you're not," Sandy growled. "But you will be."

I really should've seen the slap coming. It was becoming something of a theme, after all. Sandy hit Landon so hard she caused him to rock back on his heels. I instinctively stepped forward to protect him. "Hey!"

Sandy wasn't about to be deterred. "I know you're to blame for this. You took advantage of his amnesia and convinced him he loves you. Well, it's not true. He loves me. We're going to live happily ever after. Good always overcomes evil ... and you're evil."

"Oh, whatever."

Sandy took me by surprise when she slapped me for good measure. "Evil!"

I held my hand to my cheek as I widened my eyes and turned to Landon. "Did she just hit me?"

Landon looked as stunned as I felt. "Are you okay?" He moved closer, pulling my hand away so he could study my cheek. "Did that hurt?"

"I've been slapped before."

Thistle raised her hand. "Trust me. I've slapped her much harder than that."

"Okay, well, we're done here." Landon put his hand on the small of my back and pushed me so I wasn't close enough for Sandy to strike a second time. "We have to go. I'm sorry for your heartbreak."

Instead of issuing a threat, as I expected, Sandy dropped to her knees with an animalistic wail. "How can you do this to me? How can you abandon our love? How can you break my heart?"

"I can't even deal with this," Landon muttered.

"That's what happens when you're a heartbreaker," Marcus teased.

"Don't add to this insanity."

Landon was almost at the end of the hallway when Sandy spoke again.

"What about our baby, Jericho?"

Landon's body froze, the only movement coming from his hips as he slowly swiveled. "Excuse me?"

"I'm pregnant," Sandy announced, getting to her feet. When she hit the ground she looked like a normal, if a bit big-breasted, teenager. This time, when she stood, she was very clearly pregnant. Like ... nine months pregnant. "And you're the father."

"Oh, how is that even possible?" Landon whined. "You weren't pregnant twenty seconds ago."

"I am now." Sandy's eyes narrowed until they resembled something straight out of a horror movie. "If you think you're going to have a happily ever after with your beloved Echo Waters, think again. You might not love me, but I won't allow you to be the one who leaves."

"Oh, I've had enough of this." Landon grabbed my hand. "Come on, sweetie, we're done with this."

Curiosity kept me from strolling away. I had a feeling this scene wasn't quite finished.

"I never told you the truth about me, Jericho," Sandy hissed. "My grandmother was more than just a surgeon; she was an innovator. That means she knew how to save herself when the time came."

Landon rubbed his forehead, resigned. "I don't even want to know what's about to happen. I know it's going to suck."

"My grandmother wasn't really my grandmother when she performed her first brain transplant," Sandy continued. "She was really my grandfather, because he's the one who transplanted his own brain into my grandmother's body ... and this was long before he told anyone about the procedure because it was untested and could've led to something catastrophic."

Someone theatrically gasped, although I was fairly certain it wasn't anyone in our group. "How did he conduct his own brain transplant?" I was understandably confused.

"He was a genius. That means he had no limitations."

"That's not really what that means," Thistle pointed out. "I think there would have to be limitations on doing your own brain transplant."

"That hardly matters," Sandy said. "He did it. He put his brain in my grandmother's body. Even though it was necessary to prolong his life, he refused to be responsible for my grandmother's death. Do you know what that means?"

"That this is a stupid world," Landon answered.

Sandy ignored him. "My grandfather kept my grandmother alive, feeding her brain and hiding it in a jar so no one could see it."

"How do you feed a brain?" Sam asked. "Does it have a mouth no one knows about?"

"It's a family secret," Sandy replied. "Six months ago, I was in a car accident. You remember, right, Jericho? You sat vigil by my bedside for five whole minutes."

"I'll take your word for it," Landon said dryly.

"I was brain dead, but my grandfather kept it to himself," Sandy explained. "He had an idea."

"Oh, this is about to go to a bad horror movie place," Sam offered. "I'm just warning you now."

"My grandfather transplanted my grandmother's brain into my body, and she was finally free to reclaim her life," Sandy announced.

"If that's true, why do you keep referring to them as 'grandmother' and 'grandfather'?" Thistle asked.

"I have to keep up the ruse," Sandy said. "It's important that no one ever know."

"So that explains why you told us," Landon muttered. "Well, Sandy – or whatever your name is – that's a lovely story. I'm sorry you've been through so much."

"And now I'm pregnant," Sandy said. "How do you expect me to explain carrying your baby to my husband, whose brain is really in my old body?"

"I would suggest having a fifth of bourbon on hand when you do it," Landon replied without hesitation. "Come on, Bay. I can't listen to this ridiculous crap for one second longer. In fact ... ."

He didn't get a chance to finish, because a hilarious – although I think she was trying to be menacing – figure appeared in the doorway.

It was Margaret Little. I would recognize her anywhere. Back in Hemlock Cove she was Aunt Tillie's nemesis. Here it appeared she was going to be Sandy's grandfather ... er, grandmother ... er, I wasn't quite sure which. Ultimately it didn't matter. I knew we had to listen to that story for a reason, and the reason was standing right in front of us.

"Where do you think you're going?" Mrs. Little hissed. She looked demented, as if she'd stepped off a horror movie film reel or something. The only thing she was missing was a neon sign that declared her "batshit crazy" hovering above her head. "We're not done here."

"Oh, I can't even ... ." Landon looked weary as he dropped his forehead into his hand. "Why is this happening?"

"We really should've seen this coming," Thistle noted. "There was no way we were going to get out of this world without seeing all of Aunt Tillie's enemies. It's too much fun for her to use their likenesses when it comes to stuff like this."

"I think that means we're nowhere near being done," I said. "You just know we're going to see Aunt Willa and Rosemary before it's all said and done."

"And probably Lila, too," Clove said. "Still ... Mrs. Little makes a fabulous woman with a man's brain in her body. I think it was inspired casting."

Thistle nodded sagely. "Yes, I'm impressed, too."

"Stop talking," Landon snapped. "I don't want to be in this scene any longer. It's ridiculous. Brain transplants aren't real."

"Oh, they're real," Sandy intoned, rubbing her protruding belly. If it was even possible, she looked bigger than she had seconds before. "Our baby will be here soon, Jericho. Prepare yourself to be a father."

"I'm not watching that," Landon announced. "It's not going to happen. If that old bat thinks I'm watching this ... ."

"You watched me being born once," I reminded him. "You liked that."

"Because it was you and I didn't focus too hard on your mother's lady parts in that memory," Landon shot back. "Seeing you born was magical. Seeing whatever happens here is going to be gross, goofy and too much for me to take."

He had a point. "Okay. We'll keep going."

"Oh, you're not going to keep going," Mrs. Little announced. "I won't allow it. I have plans for all of you."

"What kind of plans?" Sam asked. "Are you going to transplant our brains, too? If so, I want to look like George Clooney when you're done."

"Oh, that's a really great choice," Clove enthused. "I love George Clooney."

"You love me more, right?"

Clove nodded without hesitation. "Absolutely."

"Stop talking!" Mrs. Little bellowed. "You're ruining the moment."

"Yeah, we're not participating in the moment," Landon announced, grabbing my hand and dragging me away from the crazy people in the center of the hallway. "We have someplace to be. It was lovely seeing the both of you. We'll have to meet for coffee eventually ... at a time far, far down the road."

"I won't let you escape," Mrs. Little shrieked, raising her hand to show off what looked to be a wicked-looking scalpel. "It's time to create a different world!"

My mouth dropped open as Mrs. Little raced forward. "Are we in a horror movie now?"

No one answered. No one had time to answer. Out of nowhere, a fissure opened in the hallway – one that barely offered any shake or sound – and Mrs. Little dropped into it before she even got close to us.

"What was that?" Landon practically exploded as he raced forward and stared into the crevice. "This is like a huge crack. It goes down hundreds of feet."

"I think this happened on *General Hospital*," Clove noted. "One of the supervillains had a son and he was hidden in a crack beneath the hospital for decades. I remember Aunt Tillie saying that she would totally like to hide her enemies in a crack beneath Hemlock Cove."

"I guess she finally got her chance," I supplied, shaking my head. "That was weird, huh?"

"You're just now getting that?" Landon challenged.

"It was totally weird," Thistle confirmed. "It was still kind of fun. Although ... is anybody worried that Aunt Tillie might really try to transplant her brain into someone else's body so she never dies? That totally sounds like something she would do."

It was a ridiculous thought, and yet ... . "We'll make sure she doesn't have any creepy brain jars in her room when we get out of this."

Thistle nodded, solemn. "Good plan."

That crazy villain lady just cursed the wedding party. It was totally cheesy and she didn't even rhyme. I still like her style.
– Aunt Tillie finds her soap opera spirit animal

TEN

Once we recovered from Mrs. Little's disappearance, we left Sandy to gnash her teeth and scream about bloody vengeance. Aunt Tillie's giggles continued until we reached the end of a hallway, and when we opened the door and stepped through it we found ourselves in an entirely different location.

Landon was baffled. "What the … ?"

I tilted my head to the side as I studied the large living room. Just to make sure, I glanced over my shoulder and found the door we'd walked through seconds before was gone.

"Apparently this is a magical soap opera world," I offered, pursing my lips. "Does anyone recognize this set?"

Thistle moved to a cabinet on a nearby wall and stared at the framed photographs on display. "No, but we're in these photos."

I moved closer, raising my eyebrows as I focused on a photo that showed Landon and me standing in front of a large building. The bricks were brown and as far as I could tell, it looked to be something of a communal apartment complex. "Hmm."

Landon looked over my shoulder. "If we're taking photographs together, how am I working undercover in this world? I don't get it."

"You're far too practical," Thistle said. "Soaps rewrite the rules whenever it suits them. If the writers kill off a character because the actor wants to leave, for example, then they simply bring him or her back through some contrived occurrence later if the actor decides he wants to return. It's a thing. You need to get used to it if you're going to adapt to this world."

"I don't want to adapt to this world. It's a stupid world."

"We still need to get through it," I reminded him. "I'm sorry about this, by the way. I'm sorry you have to go through it."

Landon's expression softened. "Bay, we've been over this a hundred times. This isn't your fault. Whenever this happens – and it seems to happen quite often these days – I don't blame you. I need you to know that."

"I do know that. It almost makes things worse, though."

"How so?"

I shrugged, conflicted. "If your mother was doing stuff like this to us, I don't think I would be as forgiving as you. I like to think I would be, but I can't see how I wouldn't get frustrated."

"I'm plenty frustrated. I'm simply not frustrated with you. Aunt Tillie did this, not you."

"I know." I rubbed my hand over my forehead. "You still have a right to be angry."

"Oh, I'm angry. I'm so angry at that woman I can barely see straight. But I'm not going to take it out on you. That's unfair, and I won't do it." Landon moved his hands to my shoulders and started rubbing. "This is as hard for you as it is for me, but there's no reason to turn on each other."

I leaned into him, thankful for a quiet moment even though I knew the storm would return ... and fast. "Thanks."

"I love you, Bay." Landon pressed a kiss to my cheek. "That won't change because you have a crazy great-aunt. I promise."

"I love you, too."

We lapsed into amiable silence and stared at the photo.

"At least we look happy," Landon said after a beat. "I still don't understand how I can bring the woman I'm supposedly having an affair with – the wife of the man I'm investigating – to an apartment complex. It makes absolutely no sense."

"You're thinking about it too hard," Marcus said. "You need to relax your brain."

"Or transplant it into someone else's head," Sam suggested.

The lame joke caused Landon to smile. "It's easier for you guys. You haven't been smacked across the face, had drinks dumped on you or had your shirt ripped off multiple times. Aunt Tillie is purposely going after me in this one."

"She always goes after you with a vengeance," Thistle pointed out. "It's one of her favorite sports. You shouldn't take it personally. It simply means she considers you an official member of the family."

"How do you figure that?"

"She always goes hardest after family. Heck, she made Clove a naughty nurse and gave me a really old husband to be mean. She gave Bay a husband who likes to pinch. She can't help herself. To her, this is fun."

"It's not going to be fun when I get my hands on her."

"Oh, I'm right there with you." Thistle's grin was evil. "That old biddy better hope I never get out of here, because if I do I'll make her pay like she's never paid before. If she thought the ants in the pants spell was bad, she ain't seen nothing yet."

"That's exactly how we ended up here," I pointed out. "She's nowhere near done with us either."

"That's downright terrifying," Landon muttered, resting his hand on my shoulder. "Okay, we're clearly here for a reason – and I doubt it's to look at photographs – so we need to split up and look around."

Sam balked. "Are you sure splitting up is a good idea?"

"Are you afraid?"

"No, I just don't want to miss whatever mistress you've got hidden in this place coming out and ripping your shirt off," Sam shot back, causing Clove and Thistle to snicker while Marcus bit his bottom lip to keep from laughing.

"Ha, ha." Landon grabbed my hand. "I don't find this funny. While I know Aunt Tillie gets her jollies out of messing with us, I'm not a cheater. I don't like it that she sees me that way."

Even though I felt he was being a bit theatrical, I couldn't help taking pity on him. "Landon, she doesn't see you as a cheater. It's just ... slapping and drink throwing are soap staples. They happen all the time."

"Yes, but they're only happening to me in this world."

"Because that's the story she built for you. I'm sorry it keeps happening. I'll try to stop the next one before she gets a chance to slap the crap out of you."

"No." Landon shook his head. "I don't want you stepping in front of me. You might get hurt."

"I've already been slapped."

"And I'm ticked about it." Landon gripped my hand tighter. "We need to figure out exactly what we're supposed to be learning here. Stay together as couples but spread out. She won't let us leave until we figure out whatever it is we're supposed to discover while in this location."

"While I agree that she wants us here for a reason, I'm not sure it's to learn something as much as play out a leg of her story," Thistle cautioned. "It's not like the fairy tale world. There aren't little life lessons knit into the seams of the narrative. This world is about her having fun. She doesn't necessarily want to teach us a lesson as much as she wants to torture us."

I hadn't really given it much thought until Thistle laid it out, but what she said made a lot of sense. "She doesn't always want to teach us. Thistle is right on that. Sometimes she simply wants to entertain herself."

"And you think that's what this is?" Landon asked.

I shrugged. I really wasn't sure. "I don't know. We need to be careful and look around. Even if she isn't teaching us something, we'll have to jump through the appropriate hoop to move on."

"Okay, let's do it." Landon tugged me close. "Be careful. We have no idea what kind of crazy person is hiding here. Given what happened in the last scene, this one could be downright deadly."

"**WOULD YOU LIKE SOME** tea and cookies?"

The woman Landon and I found when we entered the kitchen was a blast from the past.

"Edith?"

She turned, her smile pleasant and welcoming. "Did you say something, dear?"

"That might not be her name here," Landon whispered.

I nodded, understanding. I hadn't seen Edith in months. When I last saw her, she'd been a ghost. Technically, I never knew her as anything other than a ghost. She was a former classmate of Aunt Tillie's who died young. Her ghost haunted The Whistler for years, but I finally sent her on her way after the truth regarding her death came to light.

I thought when I said my goodbyes that I wouldn't miss her, and that was true. I was angry toward the end. Some of the things Edith did in life – the things that led up to her murder – were downright despicable. I was ready to wash my hands of her at the time, yet ... I couldn't deny it was good to see her.

"Do you live here?" I sat at the homey kitchen table and accepted the ornate teacup from Edith.

"It's my home," Edith replied. "I own the building and rent rooms to a variety of young men and women who are just starting out in life." She winked at Landon. "Like Jericho here. Did you know he's an undercover police officer working to take down a mob kingpin?"

Landon opened his mouth, I'm sure to say something derogatory about Jericho's undercover skills, but I shook my head to silence him.

"I heard something like that." I sipped the tea. It was good, warm and soothing going down. Whatever could be said about Aunt Tillie's worlds, I could never deny there was a certain authenticity behind them that deserved admiration. "How long have you owned this building?"

"Forever. At least I think that's how long." Edith's smile was bemused. "What are you doing here, Jericho? I thought you had a full shift at the mobster's mansion today."

"See, there's no way an undercover officer would tell his landlady that," Landon complained.

I patted his hand. "I guess it's good that you're not an undercover officer on a soap opera then, huh?"

"Yeah, yeah." Landon rolled his neck until it cracked. "I came down with a bout of amnesia so I got the day off."

"Oh, that's terrible." Edith wrinkled her nose. "I think I have a bottle of Amnesia Bismol around here. That should cure you. Do you want me to look for it?"

"Um ... ." Landon was caught off guard by the question. "Sure. Why not?"

Edith's faux smile never faded as she shuffled from the room. I waited until I was certain she was out of earshot to speak. "It's weird to see her."

Landon's hand moved to the back of my neck, his fingers working tirelessly to ease the tension there. "Does it upset you to see her?"

"I don't know. I don't know how I feel. The last time I saw her ... ."

"You haven't talked a lot about that," Landon noted. "I didn't want to push because I figured it was hard on you. If you want to talk about it, though, I'm here."

"You're always here." I sent him a warm smile. "I don't know how I feel about it. It seems somehow pointed that Aunt Tillie used her for this world, though, doesn't it? Do you think it's a dig at me?"

"Actually, I think it's the opposite."

"You do?"

Landon nodded. "I think Aunt Tillie probably wanted you to see Edith in a quiet environment."

"What if Edith turns out to be evil?"

"Then I'll have to readjust my thinking."

"Fair enough."

We lapsed into silence when we heard feet shuffling, and when Edith returned she was empty-handed.

"I could've sworn I had a bottle around, but I can't seem to find it,"

Edith supplied. "You might want to check your room, Jericho. I think you were the last one to use it three weeks ago when you had that bout of amnesia after falling off a bridge."

Landon's mouth dropped open. "I fell off a bridge?"

"Well, you were saving the woman you love from certain death thanks to a car bomb." Edith sent me a fond smile. "You were a hero. You didn't even seem to mind the amnesia."

"Oh, well, that sounds … plausible." Landon made a face. "I don't suppose you could point me in the direction of my room, could you?"

Even though he was supposed to have amnesia, that seemed an odd request. "I'm sure we can find it ourselves."

"Oh, don't be ridiculous." Edith waved off my worry. "That's what I'm here for. As a woman of a certain age, my only reason for living is to act as a sounding board to those who are younger than me. It's normal in Camelot Falls. Your room is the second on the left, Jericho. The stairs are right over there."

"Thanks." Landon drew me to my feet. "I'll bring the bottle back down if we find it."

"That sounds lovely."

I paused at the door, casting a glance over my shoulder and watching as Edith happily drank her tea, seemingly unbothered by … well … everything. "I know you won't really hear this, but I guess I've wanted to say it for a bit."

Edith looked intrigued. "And what's that, dear?"

"I'm not sorry I sent you away. I am sorry things were so bad for you at the end, though. I hope … I hope you found peace on the other side."

"I'm sure I did, dear. You shouldn't trouble yourself over such things. It makes you a kvetch, and nobody likes a kvetch."

The corners of my mouth tipped down. "Right. Well, have a good afterlife."

"Yes, yes. Enjoy your trip upstairs, dear."

This time when I turned my back on Edith I did it with a clearer conscience. Sure, it wasn't her, but I didn't feel the weight of my actions dragging me down. It was better.

"I guess this trip wasn't a total loss, huh?" Landon smiled as he led me to the second floor. "You got a little closure. That's good."

"I guess it is."

I followed Landon to the room Edith indicated, and when he opened the door I couldn't stop my laughter from bubbling up. Landon's expression revealed a mixture of fury and amazement as he scanned the room.

"You have got to be kidding me."

I don't know what I expected. In the back of my mind I thought it would be a simple room with a bed. Instead I found a round bed with a furry pink comforter, a power ballad emanating from … somewhere, and a centered disco ball swirling hundreds of hearts across the purple walls. The room looked like something straight out of a porn shoot.

"What a passion pit," I complained.

Landon took a step forward, his eyes bouncing from one side of the room to the other. "Can you believe this? Who would put a disco ball over their bed?"

"Someone who obviously gets a lot of action." I shuffled to the bed and touched the furry comforter. "This is kind of … neat. I bet it's like sleeping on top of the world's fluffiest pillow."

"It's pink."

"Well, you are a lothario in this world."

"Which I still don't like," Landon grumbled, glaring at the radio on the bookshelf when the song changed. "Criminy. Is that Nickelback again? As if things aren't bad enough."

"It's another power ballad."

"So?"

"So … this is a soap."

"So?"

He wasn't getting it and I wasn't sure how in depth I wanted to go. "Soaps are many things, Landon." I chose my words carefully. "First and foremost, they're about love in the afternoon."

Landon furrowed his brow, his face going dark before realization dawned and he widened his eyes. "You can't be serious."

"It's a seduction. We could hardly get through the world without ... you know."

Landon remained unconvinced. "Aunt Tillie is watching."

"She is, but she's not a pervert. She won't watch this. She simply wants to lead us to this."

"I'm not doing it in front of her."

I didn't have the heart to tell him the odds of us "doing it" were small. I simply knew I needed to get him in the mood to at least pretend we were going to hit the sheets. "I don't think we have much say in the matter."

"Oh, I have a choice." Landon crossed his arms over his chest. "It's not happening, Bay. There's absolutely nothing you can do to entice me to climb on that bed. Absolutely nothing."

"I bought bacon-scented bubble bath."

Landon pursed his lips. "Fine. If she sees, though, I'm going to blame you." He strode toward the bed and cupped the back of my head, the music ratcheting up a notch.

"That was a lot easier than I thought it was going to be to convince you." I was a bit breathless and my heart pounded. "I have no idea why I'm so lightheaded."

"It's the room." Landon was resigned. "It's making us do this. There can be no other explanation."

"Is that your excuse?"

"Yup."

"Okay."

Landon leaned closer. "Prepare yourself. I think this is going to be something special."

I didn't get a chance to respond, because he slammed his lips against mine and tumbled me to the bed before I could find the appropriate words.

Love in the afternoon indeed.

"**THAT WAS LITERALLY THE** worst thing that ever happened to me!" Landon bellowed as he glared at the wall ten minutes later.

I absently patted his arm. "You're okay." Unlike him, I believed I knew what was going to happen before the main event ... and I wasn't wrong.

"I'm okay? We basically just had a heavy petting session with Nickelback music. Then, at the moment we were supposed to ... you know ... the room faded to black and then we were back without music and romance. It was as if an invisible force threw a bucket of cold water on us. What's that about?"

I worked overtime to maintain my amusement. "It's a soap, Landon. It's not porn. There's no actual sex on a soap. There's just a music montage and then the moment after. That's how things work."

"I'm filing a complaint."

"With who?"

"Oh, I'll find someone."

All I could do was nod. "Okay, but I think we should head back downstairs. I'm guessing we all had an occurrence like this, and we're about to head to our next adventure."

"I've been traumatized," Landon complained, groaning as he got to his feet. "This is the worst thing that's ever happened to me. I know I said it before, but I really meant it, so I'm saying it again."

"You've been shot."

"It was still worse."

"I'll have to take your word for it."

"Oh, don't worry, I'll let you forget this."

I had no doubt he was telling the truth.

So … she's sleeping with both the father and the son? That's gross. I guess I should thank my lucky stars that she didn't add in the grandfather. Wait a second. Is that the grandfather? He looks younger than the son. He's much hotter than the others. I'm starting to think she's crazy.

– Winnie on soap opera casting decisions

ELEVEN

"I know where we have to go."
Thistle, Clove, Marcus and Sam were waiting for us at the front door when we hit the bottom of the stairs.

"And where is that?"

"An island." Thistle held up a magazine. "Check this out."

I accepted the magazine and flipped it over so I could see the front cover. Aunt Tillie smiled back from the glossy page, a huge diamond in one hand, a lewd gesture displayed with the other, and a beautiful beach behind her. The headline read "Life's Better on Witch Island."

Landon read over my shoulder. "Do I even want to know what Witch Island is?"

"I'm pretty sure it's our next destination, so we might need whatever information is in this article." I planted the magazine in his hand. "Where did you find it?"

"Our apartment."

"Oh, did you have a disco ball, too?"

Thistle shook her head. "Waterbed. Sex music. Unlimited porn."

I pressed my lips together to keep from laughing. "I see."

"No happy ending," Marcus added. "Also, it wasn't porn. It was like a sanitized version of porn. It was like porn-lite."

"You seem to know a lot about porn," Clove pointed out. "I don't think you would still be Aunt Tillie's favorite if she knew about your porn predilection."

"It's not a predilection."

"It sounds like a predilection."

"Stop saying 'predilection,'" Landon ordered, his temper flaring. "We need to focus on this stupid island. That's clearly where we have to go next. Thistle didn't stumble across that magazine by accident."

Thistle's expression was hard to read. She stared at Landon a long moment before shifting her eyes to me. "What's his problem?"

"Music montage blue balls."

"Hey!" Landon extended a finger. "We said we were never going to speak about it again."

Thistle's shoulders shook with silent laughter as Clove's cheeks turned red.

"Landon isn't a fan of the music montage," I added.

"Don't forget the bacon bath," Landon snapped. "You're totally making it up to me."

"I won't forget."

"Then let's get moving." I thought he was angry, so I was surprised – and rather pleased – when he linked his fingers with mine and tugged me toward the door. "We have an island to visit."

"How much do you want to bet it's like the world's cheesiest island?" Thistle asked as she followed. "You just know Aunt Tillie's version of Witch Island has to be completely messed up."

I nodded as we cleared the door. "But the terror is real."

IT TURNS OUT WITCH ISLAND had more in common with Coney Island than Monster Island.

"You've got to be kidding me." Landon shook his head as he stared at the strip of land across the way. It seemed the apartment complex opened to a nice view of Witch Island … and it resembled an over-the-top amusement park. "How is that an island?"

"It's surrounded by water," Thistle said dryly.

"It's surrounded by like ten feet of water on every side," Landon argued, stepping forward. He grabbed a stick from the ground and shoved it in the water, frowning when it hit bottom right away. "Like two feet of water deep to boot."

"At least we don't have to take a boat ride," Clove said philosophically. "I get seasick sometimes."

"Yes, it would be truly tragic to ride ten feet on a boat," Landon drawled. "Come on. Let's see what Witch Island holds." He gripped my hand tighter as we stepped into the water. I wasn't thrilled about getting my shoes wet, but there didn't seem to be an easier way to arrive at our destination.

Once on the other side, I took the opportunity to study the area. The spot to our right looked like an amusement park. The area to our left looked like a spa on steroids. There were mud baths, people frolicking in the mud baths, and waitresses walking around with alcoholic drinks and snacks to tempt the frolickers.

"This isn't the island on *Lost* by any stretch of the imagination," Sam noted. "It's more like a little kid's idea of what an island should be."

I shifted so I could look over my shoulder and found the apartment complex was gone. We were now literally on an island; all we could see in any direction was water. "Has anyone noticed that it's as if we're stuck in a Lego video game?"

The question caught my companions off guard.

"What do you mean?" Clove asked.

"No, she's right." Landon stared at the spot where the apartment complex used to be. "The locations are on top of each other and there are times you can only go forward instead of back. It's like a video game."

"You can roam freely in Lego video games," Sam pointed out.

"Not always, and the first time through a Lego video game you often can't go back," Landon said. "Aunt Tillie has been playing that new Marvel game the past few weeks. I've been watching her. She was complaining about not being able to roam the way she wanted. She said the people at Marvel were trying to put her on a leash."

"If only," Thistle muttered.

That sounded about right. "I don't know that it's important. I just found it interesting."

"It's another insight into how her brain works," Landon agreed. "Speaking of her brain ... ." His eyes landed on the row of amusement park games. "I don't even know what to say about this freaking island. Where do you think we should start?"

"I'm not sure." I glanced toward the romantic mud pits, quickly jerking my eyes away when I realized the couple in the nearest pit were in the middle of making out in something of a feverish way, hands and tongues flying in every different direction. "I think we should start at the amusement park."

"Why?" Landon looked to the spot where I'd stared moments before. "Oh, right. Why don't they get stopped by a music montage?"

"Because Aunt Tillie wants to use them to further torture you. Why do you think we're seeing this so soon after you were cut off from the ... loving?"

Instead of reacting with anger, Landon smirked. "She is a sadistic thing, isn't she?"

"I believe that's the top line on her business cards."

"The amusement park it is." Landon tugged so I would follow. "This place is really weird."

"Really?" Thistle rolled her eyes. "What was your first clue?"

WE STOPPED FOR THE FIRST familiar face we saw. Mrs. Gunderson, the owner of a Hemlock Cove bakery and Aunt Tillie's former friend who now served as an occasional confidant, stood behind a game booth where players had to select floating ducks to win a prize. She beamed when she saw us.

"Do you fancy a try of your luck?"

Landon slid a gaze to me. "I'm guessing this is part of the show."

"I guess." I dug in my pocket and came up empty. "Does anyone have any money?"

Everyone fruitlessly searched their pockets and offered up a series of head shakes.

"I guess we can't play," I told Mrs. Gunderson. "I'm sorry."

"Oh, you don't need money." Mrs. Gunderson's eyes gleamed. "You simply need the courage to pick a duck."

"That doesn't sound hard." Clove reached toward the tank, but Thistle slapped her hand back, earning a whine and a glare for her efforts.

"Don't," Thistle warned. "This is Aunt Tillie's game. There are consequences for everything we do. Nothing is as simple as picking a duck and getting something we want."

"She's right," Landon said. "We're risking a lot by picking a duck."

"What could we possibly risk?" Sam queried.

"I have no idea, but I wouldn't put it past her to force us into a world without bacon or something if we pick the wrong duck," Landon replied. "Or maybe she'll find a way to separate us … or something worse."

"So you don't want to pick a duck?" Mrs. Gunderson was confused. "Why come to Witch Island if you don't want to test your luck?"

"That's a good question," I said. "What can you tell us about them?" I gestured toward the mud pits, making sure to keep my eyes from focusing. No one wanted to see what was going on over there. Okay, the guys kept sneaking looks when they thought no one was watching, but they didn't openly stare or anything.

"Them?" Mrs. Gunderson arched an eyebrow. "They're dead."

"Dead?"

Mrs. Gunderson nodded. "They all died tragic deaths and left their loved ones behind. Then they were forced to wait here until the scheduled reunions."

Something about the story niggled the back of my brain, but I couldn't quite remember where I'd heard it before.

"Is this heaven?" Landon asked, his eyes drifting to the mud pits of love. "If so, I can see wanting to spend your afterlife that way."

I shot him a dirty look.

"What?" Landon held his hands palms up. "Tell me that your idea of heaven doesn't involve you, me and one of those pits, with a waitress who brings us nonstop chocolate martinis and bacon."

"It's not a terrible way to spend our afterlife," I conceded. "We're not there yet, though."

"And I'm thankful for that."

"We need to focus on the here and now."

"I am."

"Then stop leering like a pervert," I ordered. "I need to ask Mrs. Gunderson some questions, but I can't do that if I'm constantly watching you to make sure you don't get an inadvertent eyeful."

Instead of being offended, Landon barked out a laugh. "Fine. You have a deal."

"Great." I swiveled back to the game. "What do you mean they're dead?"

"They're dead," Mrs. Gunderson repeated. "One half of each super couple died in the real world and they were transported here."

"Where they met someone to frolic with in the mud?" Sam asked.

Mrs. Gunderson shook her head. "No. They're super couples. The other people in the pits are merely momentary distractions."

"Did she just explain something?" Landon asked.

"Maybe." Something clicked in my head. "I remember this. It was a *Days of Our Lives* storyline. Aunt Tillie showed us some highlights when we were kids."

"And it's important because?"

"I'm not sure."

"What do you remember about the story?" Landon was calm. "It has to play into whatever comes next."

"I remember that a lot of characters died. They were all halves of super couples or popular couples. Their loved ones were left behind to mourn, and then something happened – although I can't remember what – and somehow the other halves of the couples ended up on the island and everyone was reunited … and there was a lot of music montage sex happening."

"And that's what you think is going on here?"

"I don't know." I glanced at the nearest mud pit, cringing when I caught sight of what could only be described as vigorous ... grinding. "I don't remember it being like that."

"Aunt Tillie has them doing that because she doesn't want us to focus on them," Thistle supplied. "They're important to the story, but she doesn't want us to stare. We need to figure out why."

If anyone understood Aunt Tillie's busy brain, it was Thistle. They were so much alike it was often hard to differentiate them.

"It has to be about the couples," I said. "She's trying to warn us about something."

"What?" Landon was instantly alert. "What is she trying to warn us about?"

"I don't know."

"Is she trying to separate us?"

"I don't know."

"Is she trying to make us fight?"

"I don't know."

"Is she trying to drive me abso-freaking-lutely crazy?"

"I don't know."

"What do you know?" Landon was on edge, and I couldn't ignore his dark expression.

"I don't know what you want me to say." I purposely dragged out my words as I sucked in a calming breath. "I don't know what she has planned. It's just she rarely expends energy on something like this if it's not going to come back to bite us later."

Landon seemed to realize he was clutching me rather tightly, so he loosened his grip on my hand. "I didn't mean to yell at you."

I flashed a smile. "That was hardly you losing your temper. I've seen you much angrier than that."

"That doesn't make me feel better." Landon pressed a kiss to my forehead before swiveling to face everyone else. "We need to be careful. If the storyline she's trying to mimic here is about couples, that means she's going to do something to us ... perhaps separate us."

"What good would that do?" Sam challenged. "Isn't it more fun for her to torture us together?"

"Not if she can get her jollies by separating us." Landon gripped my hand as tightly as possible, Marcus and Sam followed suit with their respective girlfriends. "She'll enjoy separating us if she can. I think that's exactly what's going to happen very soon if she gets her way."

I wanted to argue with him, but it was fruitless. I was resigned to what was about to happen. "Landon … ."

"No." Landon extended a warning finger. "I won't be separated from you. This world is hard enough without that. I can't take it."

"I'm not sure you'll be able to stop it."

"Oh, I'll stop it." Landon puffed out his chest. "If she tries taking you from me, I swear, I'm going to sit down in the middle of this stupid island and wait for the locusts to come. I won't play the game without you."

I did my best to be diplomatic. "It's not as if we'll be separated forever."

"You sound as if you want it to happen."

"I don't, but if I work myself into a tizzy before it happens, when it does happen – and I believe that's what she's working toward – I'll start doing something embarrassing like crying. I don't want that."

"I don't want that either." Landon pulled me into his arms and gave me a long hug. "There has to be a way to make sure we don't get separated."

"The lesson is in the story," I reminded him. "She loves soaps because most of the time the couples she loves end up together. Sure, occasionally it doesn't happen because of actors and contracts, but a happy ending is the rule rather than the exception on soaps."

"And you think she's going to give us a happy ending?"

I smirked at the unintended double entendre. "I think the overblown sex fests in the mud pits are on purpose. I think the island stuff is on purpose. She knew I'd remember."

"I'm not going to give her the chance to separate us." Landon was firm as he tightened his grip on my hand, squeezing so hard he almost cut off my circulation. "It's not going to happen."

I opened my mouth, an attempt to soothe on the tip of my tongue.

As if on cue, a scream ripped through the air and drew everyone's attention to the waterfall in the distance. It wasn't overly high, but given the flat surfaces around us it looked huge on the horizon.

I gasped when I realized there was a figure falling from a high cliff into the churning waters below. "Holy ... ."

"Did you see that?" Thistle stepped up beside me. "Someone fell over that waterfall. I mean ... they freaking fell! That can't be right. That never happened on a soap, did it?"

"I think it's happened a few times." I turned back to Landon to suggest we see if we could find the person who fell, but the spot where he stood moments before was empty. I turned in every direction, even though I knew it was a waste of time, and then faced Clove and Thistle. They were equally resigned, because Sam and Marcus were missing, too.

"I knew this would happen," I groused. "I knew she'd do this."

"She warned us," Thistle noted. "You were right about that. The island was a warning."

"And what about the ducks?" I quirked an eyebrow as I turned back to Mrs. Gunderson and plucked one of the plastic floaters from the water. I flipped it over and read the message out loud. "You'll find him when your heart is ready to give up the search."

"That's a little on the nose, huh?" Thistle made a disgusted face. "I'm seriously going to strangle that old lady."

"I'm seriously going to help you."

If you were coming back from the dead, is the first thing you'd want to do is attend a wedding? I mean ... I get it. If you're married to one of the people involved in the second wedding, you probably want to stop them from being a bigamist. If they moved on that quickly, though, I would totally want them arrested.

– Twila's take on marital bliss

TWELVE

"Queenie!"

One of the guys in a mud pit – one who had another woman wrapped around him only seconds before – hopped to his feet and screamed as he looked toward the waterfall. I was so lost in thought I didn't think to look away before my retinas risked being seared by the power of his nakedness. Thankfully the dude wore a Speedo, so I didn't see anything that might scar me for life.

"Who is Queenie?" Clove asked.

"My wife." The man was beside himself. "Didn't you just see her? She went over the waterfall."

"But … how do you know it was your wife?" I was honestly interested in his answer. "That waterfall is way off in the distance. All we saw was what looked like a woman going over the falls. How can you possibly know it was your wife?"

"Hutch, aren't you coming back?" The woman the man left behind in the mud pit fixed him with a pointed and pouty look. "I'm getting cold without you to keep me warm."

"Hutch?" Thistle made a face. "Why would someone name their son Hutch?"

"I don't know, *Thistle*." I fought the urge to smirk. "The mysteries of naming children are lost on me. Of course, your name is Thistle ... something you keep forgetting."

"Oh, like Bay is better."

"Bay is much better than Thistle."

"Barely."

"Hey, we need to focus on the woman who went over the falls and the fact that we've lost our boyfriends," Clove interjected. "Besides, we all know that Bay and Thistle are stupid names. Clove, on the other hand, is a brilliant name."

"Don't make me force you into that mud pit," I threatened. "I'll bet that mud is really gross after they've been fornicating in it for hours. I'll still make you eat it."

Clove made an exaggerated face. "That is the grossest thing you've ever said to me."

"And I stand by it."

"Will you people stop talking about inane things like names?" Hutch exploded. "My wife just fell over the falls."

"What do you care?" Thistle challenged. "You were making time with the hot chick in the mud pit. You obviously didn't care about your wife."

"I'm dead."

"Are you really?" I wasn't convinced. "You look fine to me. You're well enough to get frisky in a mud pit. I've never seen a ghost do that before."

"It's therapeutic," Hutch snapped. "It opens up your pores and ... other stuff."

"Oh, yeah? What were you trying to open up with that chick crawling all over you?"

"I know!" Clove shot her hand in the air. "I know what he was trying to open with her."

"We're not playing a game of perverted Mad Libs here," Thistle supplied. "We all know what he was trying to open up with the chick."

"Hey, I don't need this abuse." The mud-covered woman scorched Thistle with a dark look. "I'm a good person."

"Yeah, we can tell." Thistle rolled her eyes. "Why are we still here? We should be moving to another location to find the guys. That's our primary concern. I say we head back toward that area behind the games and look for an exit."

"I don't think we can move to another location," I admitted. "I don't think we're finished here."

"Why?"

I shrugged. "Because a woman fell over the falls right before the guys disappeared. I'll bet they're out there searching for her. Aunt Tillie won't keep us apart for long – just long enough to torture us. She'll want us together for whatever else she has planned."

"But how do you know that we're going to meet back up here?" Clove challenged. "What if we're supposed to go to another location?"

"We would have a clue pointing us in that direction if that were the case. She's been very clear with the clues. We're not meant to leave just yet."

"So where do we go?"

I pointed toward the falls. "That way ... and I think we're supposed to take this dude with us." I turned to find Hutch making out with the woman from the mud pit. She was halfway out and perched on her elbows to make it easier for her to touch tongues with what could only be described as the grossest guy in the universe.

"Hey!" I snapped my fingers near Hutch's ear to get his attention.

"What?" Hutch's expression was sour. "What do you want? You've done nothing but yammer for the past five minutes and, quite frankly, I'm sick of it."

"That's rich coming from a guy who just watched his wife go over the falls."

Hutch blanched. "She was my true heart and soul."

"Yeah, you're doing an admirable job of mourning her," I drawled. "I'm truly astounded by the depths of your love. In fact ... you're an inspiration to us all."

Hutch bobbed his head. "Thank you."

"Wow. Apparently sarcasm isn't recognizable in the soap world," Thistle complained. "We need to escape ... and fast."

"Then let's head toward the waterfall."

"But what if the guys aren't there?" Clove's tone bordered on whiny. "I mean … what if they head in this direction?"

"Landon said he was going to sit in the center of the island and wait for you," Thistle pointed out. "He sounded serious to me."

"He was frustrated that the disco ball didn't lead to dance fever."

Thistle snorted. "He's not the only one. Marcus never complains, but I thought he was going to melt down."

"It doesn't matter what Landon says," I supplied. "It matters what he'll do. I'm sure he's complaining bitterly right now."

"I'm sure that's putting it mildly."

"He won't sit down and do nothing, though," I pressed. "He'll look for me. He'll want to find me. He won't just sit back and let me do all the work."

"But what makes you think he'll go to the falls?" Thistle asked. "How can you be sure?"

"Because he's an FBI agent. It's in his nature to investigate. While he won't be happy – and I'm sure Marcus and Sam want to throttle him right about now because his complaints are bound to be loud and vigorous – he'll go for the waterfall because that's the last thing we all saw before being separated. That's the one clue we have to go on."

Thistle looked as if she wanted to argue, but she ultimately kept her mouth shut.

"Let's go." Clove held out her hand. "I hope you're right about this."

"I hope so, too."

IT SHOULD'VE TAKEN US HOURS to hike to the waterfall. I wasn't great when it came to geography or distances – Landon often said I had a negative sense of direction – but the fact that we were standing in front of the majestic water display within twenty minutes didn't sit well with me.

"Did we find a wormhole to travel through when I wasn't looking?"

"Why are you complaining?" Clove wiped the back of her hand

over her brow to swipe away the sweat. "I'm glad we don't have to keep walking."

"That's because you're a kvetch," Thistle said, turning her attention to the raging waters at the bottom of the waterfall. "Well, we're here. I don't see Marcus, Sam or Landon."

She didn't go out of her way to sound argumentative, but I felt the sting of the unsaid accusation all the same. "They're close."

"You don't know that."

"I do. I feel it."

Thistle tilted her head to the side. It was odd seeing her with muted hair – it reminded me of when we were kids and her mother banned her from the hair dye aisle at Target after an unfortunate shoplifting incident – and for some reason it made her look younger. She looked almost vulnerable.

"Marcus is fine," I said. "Aunt Tillie would never let anything happen to him."

"I know he's fine," Thistle muttered. "I just don't want to spend time with you two when I could be with him."

Of course, even when she looked vulnerable she was often a pain in the butt. "They're close. We'll find them soon."

"You'd better be right." Thistle moved to the edge of the water and dropped to her knees to study something embedded in the soft mud. "There's a footprint here."

I looked over her shoulder. "It looks like a smaller foot."

"A woman," Thistle said. "Maybe it's Hutch's beloved wife."

"I miss her so much." Hutch's eyes were puffy and red-rimmed, even though he hadn't shed a tear during the walk. "I'll never get over her loss."

"How many times have you been married?" I asked.

"Eight. Each one was a treasure and gift."

"I figured." I rolled my neck until it cracked. "I'm sorry for your loss, but there's a very real chance that your wife survived the fall and walked off that way." I pointed toward what looked to be a small mountain. "Hey, I don't remember the island having a mountain.

When we landed, it was as flat as … well, Thistle's personality when she has a hangover."

"You'll pay for that when we get home." Thistle dusted off her hands on her jeans as she stood. "I guess we need to follow the footprints to find our next scene."

"Does anyone else think we should just hang out here?" Clove asked, splashing the cool water on her face. "It's nice and pretty. I just know wherever we're going next won't be nice and pretty."

"It sounds like an intriguing option, but we need to work through the scenes to get out of here," I reminded her. "We can't sit around and wait."

"You're very smart," Hutch intoned, leaning closer. His eyes were clear and he had a flirtatious smile on his face. "Has anyone ever told you how smart you are?"

I shifted away from him, lobbing a glare as I increased the distance between us. "Don't invade my personal space."

"That's not what I was doing." Hutch was all innocence and light. "I was merely talking about your intelligence."

"Well … stay over there when you wax poetic about what a genius I am."

"Sure. Sure." Hutch bobbed his head. "Did I mention that intelligent women turn me on? Also … I love blondes."

He made my stomach twist. "What color was your wife's hair?"

"Who can remember things like that?"

"Ugh, you're a complete and total tool." I ground my molars. "Let's go. We need to follow the footprints. Landon is probably going crazy."

"He's not the only one," Thistle said. "I kind of want to punch someone."

"I suggest Hutch."

"You read my mind."

WE WALKED ANOTHER ten minutes before the sound of voices assailed our ears. I hurried over a hill, pulling up short when I caught sight of a woman with long red hair standing in the middle of a small clearing. Behind her, a cabin materialized, making me think we'd arrived in the woods rather than remained on an island.

"Queenie?" Hutch asked, confused.

The woman turned, her eyes latching onto mine. I might not have recognized the hair – it was ridiculously red, after all – but I did recognize the face. "Lila?"

"Oh, you just knew we weren't going to make it out of here without seeing her," Thistle seethed. "Someone punch her before she gets a chance to open her mouth."

I considered arguing with the sentiment, but even a fake Lila was an annoying Lila ... and punching her in the face always held at least minimal appeal.

"Queenie, I can't believe it's you." Hutch took a hesitant step forward, his eyes glazed with unshed tears. "I thought you were dead."

"And he was really torn up about it, too," Thistle deadpanned. "For a second there we thought he might throw a party or something."

Lila didn't look nearly as happy to see Hutch as he did to see her. "I can't believe you found me. Are you stalking me? Are you trying to force me to do the one thing I don't want to do ... again?"

"I would never force you to do what you don't want to do," Hutch protested. "I love you."

"Well, I don't love you," Lila shot back. "I've found someone else. I've found my true love."

Hutch planted his hands on his hips. "And who is this rogue?"

"His name is Jericho Steele ... and he's twice the man you'll ever be."

I should've seen that coming. "Jericho? Is he here?"

"He's close," Lila replied. "He's waiting for me in there." She gestured toward the cabin. "We're going to run away together and start a new life."

"But you're pregnant with my baby," Hutch challenged.

Lila balked. "How do you know that?"

"Because I replaced your birth control pills with sugar tablets." Hutch turned aggressive. He was no longer the amiable tool hanging around a therapeutic mud pit with a woman he barely knew. He wasn't even the annoying sniffle monster who followed us to the waterfall while moaning about his probably dead wife. Now he was something else entirely. "I knew you were running around on me. I knew you were cheating. I had to stop you."

"And getting me pregnant when it was the exact opposite of what I wanted was your plan?" Lila was beside herself. "You're a fiend!"

"Oh, geez." Thistle pinched the bridge of her nose.

"I may be a fiend," Hutch shot back. "But I'm a fiend who gets what he wants, and I want you."

"Since when?" Thistle's irritation was on full display. "You had your tongue down some other woman's throat an hour ago."

"That is a lie!" Hutch roared. "I love only my wife."

I rolled my eyes. "I so don't want to be part of this conversation. Lila, where is Landon?"

Lila was confused. "Who is Landon?"

"Who is Lila?" Hutch asked.

I sucked in a breath and regrouped. "Queenie, where is Jericho?"

"I told you, he's in the cabin," Lila replied. "He's waiting for me."

I had doubts Landon would ever wait for Lila, but I was eager to be reunited with him so I moved past Lila and left her to argue to her heart's content with Hutch. Their issues were not my issues. At least I hoped they weren't my issues.

"Landon?" I waited for him to answer, but when nothing happened I tried again. "Landon?"

"Bay?"

The voice didn't come from the cabin. It came from the woods to our right. I turned in that direction, my eyes going wide when I saw Landon push his way through the trees. He was shirtless – again – but his eyes were wide and his relief, even from a hundred feet away, was palpable.

"I've been looking everywhere for you," Landon said. "Where were you?"

"Looking for you." I tilted my head to the side. "What happened to your shirt?"

Landon gestured toward Lila. "That ... beast ... happened."

"Where are Sam and Marcus?" Clove asked.

"They're right behind me. Don't worry." Landon's eyes locked with mine and his expression softened. "I was worried."

"Even shirtless again, I'm still glad to see you."

"Yeah, me too." Landon opened his arms. "Come here."

I took several steps quickly, excited to see him even though we'd been together a mere hour before. It somehow felt longer. I was only halfway to him, doing my best to ignore Lila's outraged screech, when I heard a roar and turned to the right.

I don't know what I expected. I knew it wouldn't be an easy reunion. Aunt Tillie wouldn't allow it, after all, and neither would the laws of soap operas. The thing rushing out of the woods in my direction totally flummoxed me, though.

"Bear!" Clove screeched. "Holy crap! It's a bear!"

I could see that for myself, but I had no idea what to do about it. I opened my mouth to scream, but the charging animal – its pelt white rather than black, which didn't make a lot of sense given the mountain setting – turned in my direction, lashing out with a paw and causing me to tilt to the side to avoid being swiped. I hit the ground hard, the air forced from my lungs, and I gasped when the bear turned to face me.

"Bay!" Landon panicked, and I knew he wouldn't get to me in time. Even if he did, what could he do?

I thought about casting a spell, but I had no idea what kind of spell could fight off a bear. Ultimately, it didn't matter, because another figure hurried out of the trees. I recognized this one after two quick blinks. Aunt Tillie wore a red, white and blue sequined evening gown. She also had a headband that looked as if it was lifted from the Statue of Liberty's head, and a determined look on her face.

"Aunt Tillie?"

She didn't bother looking in my direction, instead stepping in front of the bear and doing the one thing no one expected. She lashed out with her hand and slapped the bear across its snout, causing it to rear back and howl as if it had been hit by a car.

"Don't even think about it," Aunt Tillie bellowed. "I'm Alexis Kane, and I won't stand for any nonsense in my story. Don't you ever forget that."

And just like that, Aunt Tillie scared off a bear with a slap ... and we'd discovered a completely new level of insanity.

I've given it a lot of thought and I have a plan for explaining why I was seen hiding outside of Margaret Little's shop even though I told Terry I was in my greenhouse. I have an evil twin. No. Really. Think about it. It's perfect. Now I have someone to blame everything on and no one can prove it's not true because we look exactly the same. It's genius ... and I'm only sorry I didn't think of it sooner.

– Aunt Tillie promoting the merits of an evil twin

THIRTEEN

"**B**ay!" Landon didn't pay the bear any heed as he skirted around the creature's massive bulk and ran to my side. He didn't pull me in for a hug, as I expected, instead running his hands over my head, back and shoulders as if he was frantically looking for wounds to bandage.

"Are you okay? Did you get bit? Do I have to kill Aunt Tillie right here and now?"

I arched an eyebrow as I looked between him and Aunt Tillie. "I'm fine."

"Well, I'm not fine." He gave in and pulled me close for a hug. "I'm pretty freaking far from fine."

I absently patted his back and glared at Aunt Tillie. "You are in so much trouble."

Aunt Tillie was blasé. "I have no idea what you're talking about. By the way, I just saved you from a bear."

"A polar bear," I grumbled, giving the bear – which had seemingly lost interest in attacking – a wide berth as I stood. Landon dusted off my jeans, his hands shaky. "I take it you stole the polar bear from *Lost*."

"I am Alexis Kane," Aunt Tillie intoned. "I don't steal from anything or anyone. I am an original."

"You're ... something." I grabbed Landon's hands, which were becoming progressively more obsessive as he worked to clean off my clothing. "I'm okay. I can't die in this world. Aunt Tillie wouldn't allow that."

"I know, but ... it was a freaking bear."

"It was definitely a bear." Thistle, her fingers linked with Marcus' trembling digits, approached with a wary look. It seemed I wasn't the only one who had a nice, albeit stressful, reunion with my significant other. "And you totally stole that from *Lost*, you old crone."

Aunt Tillie sniffed, disdainful. "If you think I'll allow you to talk to me in that manner, you have another think coming."

"Yeah, yeah." Thistle brushed off the warning with a wave of her hand. "We're ready to go home."

"Yeah, you've had your fun," Clove said, Sam pressed to her back as they appeared to our left. "Send us home."

"I'm sure I have no idea what you're talking about," Aunt Tillie supplied. "I've never seen you people before."

I narrowed my eyes as I licked my lips. The woman standing before us could be Aunt Tillie. It looked like her. Aunt Tillie was known to appropriate her own image at times, though, so it was equally possible this was simply another clone like the ones we'd seen of other acquaintances and loved ones along our endless journey.

"Now you listen here ... ." Landon grabbed the front of Aunt Tillie's sequined dress and lifted her a good foot off the ground as he stared into her furious eyes. "We want to go home. You've gotten more than enough jollies for one night. Quite frankly, I don't know why you consider this fun, but you've had plenty of it.

"We've been good sports," he continued. "I've been slapped so many times I've lost count. I've lost my shirt so many times I can't even remember what I was wearing when we first landed. Enough is enough."

"You have to send us home," Clove added, her voice plaintive. "We don't want to be here any longer."

The look Aunt Tillie shot Clove was straight out of a bad movie. "I don't know you. I've never seen you before. I can tell right away you're a total kvetch, though. Alexis Kane does not suffer kvetches."

"Oh, good grief." Thistle sank to the ground, glaring at the bear as it eyed her with what looked to be hunger. "Don't even think about it. I'll bite you back, and I have rabies so it won't end well for you."

I pursed my lips to keep from laughing. "Aunt Tillie ... ."

"I've never heard of this Aunt Tillie you speak of." Aunt Tillie's tone was forced and clipped. She sounded like a snotty rich woman on an eighties soap opera. Technically, of course, that's what she was going for, so she managed to do it with aplomb. "My name is Alexis Kane."

"Ugh. It's like talking to a wall." Thistle flicked her eyes to me. "We could wrestle her down and poke her with needles – or knives, if we can find them – until she gives in. We could see if our magic works enough to curse her into submission. Or, and I'm just spitballing here, we could take her back to the waterfall and throw her over."

"That waterfall is lethal," Lila interjected. "I only survived because I was determined to get back to my love." She batted her eyelashes at Landon, who quickly looked in the opposite direction. "Love kept me alive, Jericho. That love will continue to sustain me."

"It's still wrong to punch women in a soap opera world, right?" Landon looked weary when he pinned me with a gaze. "I know she's not real, but ... ."

"You can't hit my wife," Hutch snapped. "She's pregnant with our child."

"Only because you switched out my birth control pills." Lila's eyes fired. "You wanted to keep me from my heart, but it won't work." Lila scrambled to get around Hutch and threw her arms around Landon's neck before he could evade her. "Tell him, Jericho. Tell him we're meant to be together."

"Oh, why is it always me?" Landon whined as he tried to extricate himself from Lila's grip. "Why isn't this happening to Sam and Marcus, too?"

"Because you're the leading man." I answered before I thought better of it.

"What is that supposed to mean?" Landon grabbed Lila's wrists and positioned her so she was in front of him but couldn't run her fingers through his hair. Under normal circumstances I would've been offended, infuriated even. Now I was too tired to muster outrage.

"She means that you're the leading man." Thistle wrinkled her forehead. "That suggests she's the leading heroine and Clove and I are supporting characters."

Crap. This wouldn't end well. "That's not what I said."

"But you're thinking it."

"I am not."

"You are so."

"I am not."

"You are so."

"I am not."

"Okay, as much as I would like to wait it out and see how many times you guys can say that to one another, it's not helping," Marcus chided. "We won't get through this if you guys start arguing."

I stretched my arms over my head. "I'm not the one who started the fight."

"Of course not," Thistle sputtered. "You're the leading lady. You're above a fight."

"I didn't say I was the leading lady!"

"Knock it off." Landon moved away from Aunt Tillie, although the look he shot her over his shoulder threatened potential mayhem if she attempted to flee. "I don't see why you're arguing about this. Who cares about the leading lady designation?"

Thistle, Clove, Lila and Aunt Tillie shot their hands in the air in unison.

"I'm the leading lady," Lila said. "I'm propelling the story right now. I mean ... my husband tricked me into getting pregnant, I just fell over a waterfall and the love of my life is grappling with the fact that I'm carrying another man's child. How am I not the leading lady?"

"Don't refer to him as 'the love of your life,'" I snapped.

"Are you jealous?"

"No, I just don't like it."

"I'm with Bay." Landon slipped an arm around my shoulders and glared at Lila. "I am not the love of your life. Stop saying that. It makes us all uncomfortable."

"It doesn't make me uncomfortable," Aunt Tillie countered. "Besides, I'm the leading lady."

Thistle snorted. "You can't be the leading lady. Soaps are ageist. Once you hit forty you became the matriarch, not the leading lady. I'm the leading lady, for the record. We all know it."

"You aren't the leading lady," Clove argued. "You're too mean to be the leading lady. You're the sidekick, the comic relief. You're occasionally used for a plot device or to make someone pay. The leading lady can't be mean."

"And I suppose you think you're the leading lady," Thistle said dryly.

Clove folded her arms over her chest and lifted her chin. "It makes the most sense."

"How do you figure?"

"Bay is too boring to be the heroine," Clove replied. "You're too mean. That leaves me. I'm perfect. I'm cute. I'm a good person. I can cry without thinking about it. I'm obviously the leading lady."

Wait a second … . "I'm too boring to be the leading lady? That's a bunch of hogwash."

"You're not boring, sweetie." Landon patted my shoulder. "You're perfectly fine the way you are. In fact, I think you're the least boring person in the world."

I stared at him for a long moment. "You know you have lipstick on your chin, right?"

Landon's hand automatically flew to his face. "What?"

"Yeah. It just so happens to match Lila's lipstick."

"That's my lipstick," Lila corrected.

"That's what I just said."

"My name is Queenie."

"Ugh, I'm so sick of the ridiculous names in this world," I complained. "I can't tell you how annoying these names are."

"Tell me about it," Hutch lamented. "You'd think people would have better names."

"Yeah, *Hutch*," Thistle said dryly. "You're definitely the person who should be complaining about stupid names."

Hutch was placid. "I thought so, too."

"Ugh." Thistle slapped her hand to her forehead. "This place is stupid. You know what? I don't care that I'm not the leading lady. I can live with that if we get out of here."

"Thank you." Clove bobbed her head. "I'm glad you see things my way."

Thistle snorted. "You're not the leading lady. You might as well get over that right now. Aunt Tillie set this up so Bay is the leading lady and that means Landon is the hero. That's why he has a woman in every port, so to speak."

"Yes, it's a lovely development," I agreed, glaring at the pink lipstick on his chin.

"I didn't kiss her." Landon swiped at his face again. "She threw herself at me. I, being a loyal boyfriend, explained that I wanted nothing to do with her." He looked to Marcus and Sam for support. "Tell her."

"Oh, we're your sidekicks," Sam drawled. "How can we possibly know the motivations of the leading man?"

Landon looked desperate. "Bay … ."

I held up my hand to still him. "I know you didn't kiss her. Trust me. No one would want to kiss that frog."

"Hey!" Lila was affronted. "Jericho and I are in love."

"Stop saying that," Landon ordered. "It gives me a sour stomach."

"Oh, well, if that's how you want to be." Lila reared back and slapped Landon across the face, putting as much effort as possible behind the blow. Landon barely reacted. "You've broken my heart and I hope you know I'm going to make you pay."

Hutch brightened. "You tell him, baby! Does that mean you're coming home with me?"

Lila didn't look thrilled at the prospect. "I guess, but I hear they're hiring a new actor soon and I'm sure he's going to be my new love interest. This is only temporary."

Hutch wasn't about to be dissuaded. "That's okay. I'll just get you pregnant again."

"I'm already pregnant."

"Who doesn't love twins? Besides, if you have twins, it's far more likely one of them will eventually die and you'll get bumped up to leading lady when that happens."

Lila pursed her lips and nodded. "Good idea."

"Oh, I hate these people." Thistle was disgusted. "I just ... this is the dumbest world we've ever been to."

"I kind of like it," Clove said. "The music is great, and who doesn't love a good montage?"

Landon, Marcus and Sam raised their hands.

"Montages suck," Landon said. "That's still the worst thing that's ever happened to me."

"You'll survive." I squeezed his wrist. "We need to find you another shirt. Even though Lila has backed off, she keeps glancing over here. I think she might be drooling."

"If she touches me again I expect you to fight her off." Landon was somber. "She makes my skin crawl."

The simple declaration was enough to warm my heart. "Thank you." I kissed his cheek. "Now, Aunt Tillie, I think we've been good sports. It's time you sent us home." I turned to the spot where she'd stood only moments before and found it empty. "Aunt Tillie?"

"I told you there's no one here by that name." Aunt Tillie's voice echoed throughout the clearing – as if amplified by megaphone – and when I turned to the cabin I found she'd managed to move a good distance away. The bear was gone, but two shadowy figures had joined the fray, bracketing Aunt Tillie. Unfortunately, they looked exactly like her.

"Oh, holy moly," Clove complained, dumbfounded disbelief washing over her face. "There are three of her. How is that even possible?"

"The world is surely coming to an end," Thistle complained. "Three Aunt Tillies? Someone just needs to smite me now."

"I'll do it," Lila offered.

"Don't you have someplace else to be?" Thistle shot back. "No one was talking to you."

"I'll do it," Clove volunteered.

"I hate all of you." Thistle made a disgusted face as she focused on the trio of Aunt Tillies. "What's this? Are we back to science fiction? Is Aunt Tillie cloning herself?"

That was a very good question. "I don't think so. I think it's supposed to be a take on twins or dual roles."

"Oh, so she's triplets instead of twins because Aunt Tillie has to beat everyone," Thistle mused. "That makes sense."

"You have no idea the power you're messing with," Aunt Tillie's Alexis Kane persona uttered dramatically. "We're stronger than you."

"You're ... something," I agreed. "We still want to go home."

"The story isn't done."

"It is for us."

"And yet it's not." Aunt Tillie's smile was bright. "I don't believe I've gotten the chance to introduce my sisters. This is Nikki Forrester and Marlena Bauer. They're my more evil and most evil twins."

"Oh." Realization dawned. "We really should've seen that coming."

"Wait ... more evil and most evil?" Landon was understandably confused. "How does that work?"

"One does the work of the more evil me and the other does the work of the most evil me."

"So you're evil," Thistle said, pointing. "She's more evil and that one is the most evil?"

Aunt Tillie nodded.

"Oh, that's somehow diabolically spot on," Thistle said. "That's so ... her."

"I want a more evil twin," Clove complained. "That would really help when there's housework to be done."

I ignored her. "Aunt Tillie, where do you think you're going?" I challenged. "We're here. We can see you. We won't allow you to escape again."

"That's right," Thistle enthused. "We want to go home, and we want to do it right now."

"Oh, but the story isn't over." Aunt Tillie's eyes gleamed as she took a backward step toward the cabin. We're nowhere near done."

"Where are you going?" Alarmed, I strode forward. The two twins moved into my path, blocking Aunt Tillie from view as she opened the cottage door.

"If she goes inside we'll lose her until we hit another scene," Landon warned.

"It's too late," I said. "We can't get to her in time."

"We have to try." Landon gripped my hand and broke into a run, dragging me forward. The evil twins tried to stop us, but Landon easily evaded them with a spin move straight off a football field.

"I think we pinned down why he's the leading man," Sam said, his chest heaving as he struggled to keep up. "That was a nice move, man."

Landon was grim. "I do my best." He shoved open the door and pushed his way inside, revealing an entirely new atmosphere. "Oh, I just knew it!"

We definitely weren't out of the woods yet. The new set was something else entirely.

"Oh, this doesn't look good," Thistle complained. "She's just messing with us now. There can be no other explanation."

How can you solve a crime shirtless? What kind of cop goes to a scene shirtless? Why is that dude always shirtless? If your answer is 'because he's hot,' I think we're going to have to break up. This is not proper crime scene etiquette.

– Landon trying to understand soap opera crime-solving techniques

FOURTEEN

"Where are we now?"

Landon looked over his shoulder to see if the cottage remained, but it was gone, replaced by a dark and grimy alley wall. Er, well, rather the sort of wall a soap opera pretended was dark and grimy. Alleys and docks, overall dark locations, never looked as they should in the real world when translated for the small soap screen. Apparently soap lovers could only accept so much grit.

"I'm guessing we're in an alley," Clove offered sagely.

Landon offered a withering expression. "Really? I never would've figured that out myself. Thank you so much for deducing that, Clove."

"You're welcome."

I grabbed Landon's arm and dragged him to the right, pointing toward a clothesline stretching across the back corner as I attempted to distract him. Several items of clothing hung from it, and because Landon remained shirtless I figured he might want to cover up.

"Good eye, sweetie." Landon grabbed the nearest shirt. It was purple and silky. He looked a bit like a gigolo when he shrugged into it, but he seemed so relieved to cover his chest that I opted not to comment on the color – or texture – or the ridiculous flare of the collar. Thistle was another story entirely.

"You look like a total tool."

Landon scowled. "I didn't pick out the shirt. It's not as if I have many options."

"Is that silk?" Sam stroked Landon's chest, earning a glare for his efforts. "It's … nice."

"He looks like a pimp," Thistle argued.

Landon shifted his eyes to me. "What do you think?"

I wasn't sure what to think. "I don't know." I ran my hand over his chest, resting it on top of his heart and smiling. "The color is nice on you. The silk is a bit much. I actually prefer the bare chest, but I can tell you're starting to feel self-conscious. I don't think it's that bad."

Landon rested his hand on top of mine, keeping it where it was so I could feel the steady beat of his heart. "I like being shirtless just fine … when it's you and me alone. Solving crimes and fighting enemies shirtless is just … not how I work."

"It's how soap Landon works."

"Yes, well, I think Jericho is a moron." Landon took me by surprise when he leaned forward and kissed my forehead. "How are you holding up? We didn't get a chance to talk about what happened while we were separated."

"Nothing much happened on our end. We talked to that loser Hutch. We went to the waterfall. We found a footprint. We went to the cabin. That's it."

"That's not nearly as bad as I imagined." Landon swayed back and forth, his arms loose around me, the motion somehow soothing. "I was worried about you."

"Funnily enough, I wasn't worried about you. I knew you'd be okay."

"Lila tried to kiss me. That's pretty far from okay."

"Yet you survived. We're together again." I pressed the side of my head to his chest and briefly shut my eyes. "I'm tired. I know we're really in our bed at The Overlook, sleeping, but I'm tired all the same."

"That's because this is a busy world." Landon stroked my hair. "How much longer do you think we'll be stuck here?"

"Until we reach the end of the story."

"And there's no hope for reprieve, right? She won't let us off early for good behavior, will she?"

I chuckled, amused. "Have you ever known Aunt Tillie to give up before she gets the outcome she wants?"

"No, but ... I guess I was trying to delude myself that we would be out of this soon."

"I don't believe we have terribly long left here, but I also don't think we're close to being done yet. She built a continuous story. You know darned well she'll be the star when we get to the end."

"Yeah, I think we all know that." Landon kissed the corner of my mouth and then released me. "Let's see what fresh hell she's stirred up for us next, huh?"

I nodded and turned back, pursing my lips when I saw Thistle's glare. "What?"

"I can't believe you guys are the leading couple," Thistle complained. "Clove was right. You're boring. That thing you guys just did? Yeah, it was boring."

I heaved out a sigh. "I'm more than willing to cede my leading lady title if it means Marcus will be the one getting slapped around from here on out. Maybe he'll have his shirt ripped off for a change. How does that sound?"

"I'm fine with it," Thistle replied. "Marcus looks smoking hot without a shirt."

"Are you saying Landon doesn't?"

Thistle shrugged. "I just happen to think Marcus looks better ... and I've seen both of them thanks to this little trip."

Now it was my turn to frown. "I'm pretty sure Landon looks better without his shirt on."

"Oh, thank you, sweetie," Landon drawled. "I'm so glad you picked this to fight about and not my honor when Lila was throwing herself at me."

I ignored the dig. "Marcus is nice, but Landon is better."

Thistle's eyes flashed with anger at the same moment the sky illuminated with faux lightning. Thistle and I turned away from each other at the same time, our potential fight forgotten as we stared at the sky.

"Did you see that?" Thistle narrowed her eyes. "It's like lightning except ... it's not."

"It's a lightning effect," Sam supplied. "I know because I've been considering doing similar things for the barge this upcoming season. I want to be able to simulate thunderstorms. I think the guests will really enjoy it."

"So it's not really a storm," Landon mused. "We're not really outside, are we?" He lifted his head and stared at the black sky. There was no ceiling there, and yet it was obvious we were in an enclosed space of some sort. "How come we're not outside?"

"I told you when this first started that soap sets were minimal," I reminded him. "That's what we're dealing with here."

"What else are we dealing with?" Thistle asked, turning to face an ornate door with a series of runes carved into the frame. "Look at these."

"What are they?" Landon moved close to me. "Do you know what those are?"

I shrugged. "They look relatively familiar. I'm sure they're from some book or another."

"Witch book?"

"Wiccan, but sure." I flashed him a smile. "She put these symbols here to signify the shift in the story. I don't think it's a coincidence that she picked runes to mark this door. It's a warning of sorts."

"What kind of warning?"

"We're heading into a paranormal world when we open this door."

Landon stilled. "Isn't the whole world paranormal?"

It took me a moment to realize what he was getting at. "Yes ... and no. Aunt Tillie is using magic to make us believe we're in a different world where the rules of soap operas are key. The world itself is fairly normal, at least in the grand scheme of things."

"She's saying that this isn't a magic world," Thistle added. "It's not as if Aunt Tillie shoved us into a horror world where different kinds of magic might be at play. It's not even a scientific world, so we can't use Bay's ridiculous amount of *Star Trek* knowledge."

I balked. "Hey! *Star Trek* rules."

"Yeah, yeah." Thistle rolled her eyes. "The most important thing is that this world has mostly followed real-world rules. Sure, people come back from the dead here and we have evil, more evil and most evil triplets, but the laws of life still hold true."

"What aren't you telling me?" Landon prodded.

"Not all soaps follow the same rules," I replied. "Not all soaps are created equal."

"Meaning?"

"Meaning that there were three soaps that created their own rules and featured paranormal creatures," Clove supplied. "*Dark Shadows* was the original. It had an intricate vampire storyline."

"Are you telling me that we'll be dealing with vampires in this scene?" Landon was incredulous. "Soap opera vampires?"

I held my hands palms out and shrugged. "I really don't know. *Passions* had a witch."

"And a doll that came to life, but that was altogether creepy," Thistle said. "I don't want this to turn into *Passions*. *Dark Shadows* is better."

"You said there were three supernatural shows," Marcus prodded. "What's the third?"

"*Port Charles*."

"And what's wrong with *Port Charles*? I can tell something is wrong by the looks on your faces."

"*Port Charles* was simply a really odd mixture of things," I replied. "Vampires, vampire slayers, angels – other things. It was completely loopy and crazy. Plus, it was set in the same city as *General Hospital*, but the characters there never commented on the paranormal aspects being highlighted on *Port Charles*. It was simply … weird."

"Isn't that the status quo for all soaps?"

"Not like this."

"I don't even want to see what's on the other side of this door." Landon rubbed his forehead. "I just know this is going to suck."

"Vampires suck," I agreed, smirking when Thistle and Clove broke into giggles. "Shall we?" I gestured toward the door.

"Let's do this." Landon put his hand on my lower back. "I can't wait to see who rips my shirt off in this world. I hope it's a witch."

"That sounds lovely," I muttered.

He lowered his mouth to my ear. "I hope it's my witch."

I didn't want to smile, but I couldn't help myself. "I don't think you're going to get that lucky."

"I guess we'll just have to wait and see."

INSIDE WAS BETTER THAN outside, but only from a clinical perspective. It was supposed to look grimy, but instead it looked like a video game version of Dracula's tomb.

"Oh, well, this is lovely." Landon grabbed my hand and pulled me closer to his side. "Is that a coffin?" He gestured toward the center of the room with his chin.

I nodded. "Yup. A coffin with a moon roof to allow stardust to land on it." I moved closer, but Landon wasn't happy with my curiosity and pulled me back.

"What are you doing?"

"Looking inside."

"Are you joking?"

"Does it look like I'm joking?"

"Why would you possibly want to look inside of a coffin?" Landon challenged. "No good can come of that."

"If we don't, we'll never get out of here."

"She's right." Thistle moved ahead of us. "I'll do it."

"I think that's a good idea," Landon said after a beat. "It's your turn to be the leading lady. That means you get to open the casket. We'll stay right here and watch your back."

Thistle made a disgusted face. "Whatever." She strolled to the edge of the coffin, looked around to make sure someone wasn't about to jump out of the shadows and attack her, and tugged open the heavy lid. The figure inside threw me for a loop.

"Chief Terry?" I broke free of Landon's grip and hurried to the coffin, leaning forward when I saw the familiar face. "Is he ... dead?"

"It's not real, Bay," Landon reminded me, appearing at my elbow. "That's not really Chief Terry."

"I know, but ... ."

Chief Terry, who had been still as granite moments before, flicked open his eyes and pinned me with an unreadable look. "Who are you?"

His voice was chilling, as was the echo that filled the room.

"Why does he echo, but we don't?" Clove asked, looking around.

"Because he's a vampire, stupid," Thistle chided. "Vampires echo."

"Since when?" Clove's annoyance came out to play. "I don't ever remember vampires echoing in movies and stuff. In fact, the vampires in *Twilight* didn't echo."

"That's because the vampires in *Twilight* weren't real," Thistle shot back. "They were weak little brooders who sparkled. Those aren't vampires. They're Las Vegas showgirls."

She had a point. "Chief Terry, what are you doing in there?" I peered over the coffin edge even though Landon kept trying to drag me back. "I don't think you should be in there. That can't be good for your back."

Chief Terry smiled, the expression slow and seductive. His fangs gleamed under the moonlight and made my stomach twist. Even though I knew it wasn't real, I didn't like it. "I am the king of the living dead. I don't suffer ... back pain." He rolled to a sitting position, groaning as he rubbed his lower back. "See. I'm a king."

"You're also wearing a cape." Landon relaxed a bit when he saw Chief Terry's outfit up close. "You look like Batman."

Chief Terry rolled his eyes. "I'm king of the living dead."

"Shouldn't that be undead?" Thistle asked, fingering the cape. "Polyester, huh? Aunt Tillie should've spent a little more money on costumes."

"I have no idea who this Aunt Tillie you speak of is."

"Alexis Kane," I supplied. "She's supposed to be a big deal around these parts."

"Alexis Kane is the queen of everything," Chief Terry explained. "She is not part of the living dead team. In fact, she tries to kill our kind. We're at war."

"Of course you are." Landon smiled as he patted Chief Terry's head. "Mousse, huh? Your hair is a bit crispy."

"Of course it is," Thistle said. "Vampires have to slick back their hair. It's one of the rules."

"Edward Cullen didn't," Clove protested.

"Don't bring up that name again," Thistle warned. "He's not a real vampire."

"There's no such thing as vampires," Landon scoffed. "This is an Aunt Tillie thing. It's kind of fun. You should stand up so we can see the full cape effect, Terry."

"We don't know that vampires aren't real," Clove countered. "Just because we've never seen one doesn't mean they're not real."

Landon looked to me. "Tell her they're not real."

"Well ... ." I chewed my bottom lip. "She's not technically wrong. We don't know that vampires aren't real."

"Come on." Landon was annoyed. "You guys are just messing with me now."

"We're not," I countered. "We're ... simply telling it like it is. We don't know if vampires are real. We've gotten conflicting reports while growing up."

Landon glanced at Thistle. "Surely you don't believe in vampires."

"I don't know what I believe," Thistle replied. "The thing is, I'll bet you didn't believe in witches a year and a half ago. How did that work out for you?"

Landon balked. "That's completely different."

"How?"

"Because ... well ... because there's a perfectly good reason for witches to exist," Landon replied. "You guys are magical, but not dead or anything. Vampires are dead."

"Undead," Sam said.

"Living dead," Chief Terry corrected. "We're living dead. Zombies are undead. They have their own little part of the story."

My shoulders tensed. "This story?"

Chief Terry's smile was mischievous – and a bit evil. "Another story. You won't get to play in that world today."

"Thank the Goddess for small favors," Clove muttered.

"As for me, I'm king of the vampires," Chief Terry said. "You must do what I say."

"And what is that?" Landon wasn't in the mood to mess around. "What must we do? Whatever it is, it had better be quick. I have a proper hangover to get to and it won't happen in this world."

Chief Terry stared at him for a moment. "Do you really want to know?"

"That's why I asked."

"Well then ... ." Chief Terry moved to climb out of the coffin, sweeping his arms out so the cape flowed around him. Instead of moving with grace and agility, he tripped over the cape as he tried to clear his escape and pitched forward. He hit the ground face first, groaning as his forehead smacked into the pavement. "Ow."

"I'm guessing that's not how that was supposed to go," Landon said dryly.

"I will make you join my living dead army if you're not careful," Chief Terry warned. "I won't give you a good job, either. I'll make you a janitor or something. How do you like that?"

"As long as I can wear a shirt I'm fine with it." Landon grabbed Chief Terry under his arms and hauled him to his feet. "So, where are we going?"

"To a wonderful new place." Chief Terry smoothed his cape. "Follow me."

We fell into step behind him as he crossed the room.

"Does anyone else think Aunt Tillie's version of vampires is ridiculous?" Clove asked. "I mean ... he doesn't fly or anything."

"I think we should be thankful that things turned out this way and leave it at that," Landon said. "Things could be so much worse."

I stopped abruptly, grimacing when Thistle smacked into me. I leveled a dark look at Landon, though he didn't look bothered by my fury.

"What?"

"You totally jinxed us," I barked. "Now that you said that, wherever Chief Terry is taking us will be all kinds of awful. Why would you do that?"

Landon shrugged. "I don't know. It just slipped out. Things will be fine. Don't have a fit for no reason."

I wanted to believe him, but I knew darned well things weren't going to be fine. "When this blows up in our faces, I'm totally going to blame you."

"That seems more than fair."

How many times has that dude been married? It's in double digits now, right? Why wouldn't they stop issuing marriage licenses and for the love of all that's holy, why would anyone marry him? His wives keep ending up dead, and you just know he's not paying alimony to the few who survived. It's ridiculous.

– Thistle on soap opera romance

FIFTEEN

Chief Terry kept spouting nonsense – I couldn't wait to tell him about Aunt Tillie's take on his vampire persona when we were out of this mess – as he led us through a series of winding hallways. His vampire knowledge was immense – and straight out of a series of bad books and television shows.

"I'm the first of my kind," Chief Terry explained. "I came here because I wanted peace and solitude. I found something else."

"And what was that?" Landon asked, keeping a firm grip on my hand. The shadows on either side obviously made him nervous. He scanned the darkness with each step to make sure nothing jumped out and attempted to devour us.

"I found my destiny."

Landon made a rueful face. "When I tell the real Terry how you're acting, he'll be mortified. I'm never going to let him live it down. I'm going to bring it up from now until eternity."

"I have no idea what you're talking about." Chief Terry paused in front of an ornate door. This one was white and decorated with bright flowers. It almost looked festive despite the murky lighting. "I am who I have always been."

"Yeah, the real Terry is going to toss Aunt Tillie in jail for this one."

Landon looked thrilled at the prospect. "I hope he throws away the key. I hope he makes her eat gruel and never allows her to watch soaps again. That should be her punishment."

"That sounds nice." I was trying to appease him, even though I knew it would never happen. "I'll bring it up to him at breakfast ... if we ever get to breakfast, that is."

"Oh, we'll get there. I can see it already. Blueberry pancakes. Eggs. Hash browns. Mountains of bacon. We're definitely getting to breakfast."

As if on cue, his stomach growled. I smiled as I pressed my hand to his flat abdomen. "Hungry?"

"I want out of here," Landon clarified. "That's what I want more than anything."

"Well, let's see what's next for us."

Chief Terry opened the door and gestured for us to go through it. Marcus, Sam, Thistle and Clove kept their heads down as they passed over the threshold. Landon stopped in front of Chief Terry long enough to give his outfit another appraising look.

"I wish we could take photographs here."

A small woman wearing a red suit and a bright smile poked her head through the open door. I didn't recognize her, but she seemed to know us. "Photographs will be available at the end of the show. They'll be in the gift shop and they're priced for bulk copies."

"Oh, well ... ." Landon licked his lips. "Okay then." He turned to me. "Did you hear that? There's a gift shop."

"Maybe we can get you another shirt."

Landon didn't look happy at the prospect. "Keep it up." He lifted his eyes to Chief Terry's face. "What's next?"

"I don't know. I can't go with you."

"Why?"

"You'll see. I'm not part of that story," Chief Terry explained, his eyes snagging with mine. Even though he was supposed to be a vampire – sure, he was a weak and weird vampire, but a bloodsucker all the same – he looked almost fond when he tucked a strand of my hair behind my ear. "I'm sorry you can't stay. You'd make an excellent minion."

It should've been an insult, but my insides warmed all the same. "That's probably the nicest thing anyone has said to me since I got to this insane world."

"Hey, I've told you that I love you at least three times," Landon complained.

"You know what I mean." I instinctively gripped Chief Terry's hand, marveling at its coolness. "Why do you think she showed you to us at all?"

Chief Terry was confused. "Who?"

"Aunt Tillie. I mean, Alexis Kane. Why do you think she led us to you? You know she did that, right?"

Chief Terry shrugged. "I have no idea. Alexis does what she wants, when she wants and how she wants. She's all knowing, all powerful and the one person in this world I fear."

"That definitely sounds like something that she would make you say," Landon said.

I gave Chief Terry's hand a squeeze and then released it. "I'll make sure the real you knows she made you say that. You might want to get a little retribution for that one."

"Okay. I'm sorry you're not my minion."

I cracked a smile. "I'm kind of sorry I didn't get to be a vampire for a bit, too."

Wow! There's something I thought I would never say, let alone mean.

LANDON AND I LANDED IN a church vestibule on the other side of the door. There was no sign of the others, but the woman who notified us about the gift shop stood in the center of the room with a clipboard.

"This is ... extravagant," Landon noted as he stared at the ceiling. "This is a big freaking church."

"It is," I agreed. "I wonder why we're here."

"You're here for your wedding, of course," the woman said. "Now ... come along. We're behind schedule already. You need to get dressed and ready."

I was dumbfounded. "I'm sorry, but ... what?"

"Yeah, what?" Landon almost sounded as if he was suffocating. Clearly the announcement freaked him out more than it did me.

"You're getting married," the woman repeated.

"Are you sure?"

"Of course I'm sure. You hired me as your wedding coordinator."

"Oh, well ... ." I looked to Landon for guidance but he seemed lost in his own little world. "You'll have to excuse me, ma'am. I'm a little flustered. You know ... nerves. Can you remind me of your name?"

"Of course. It's Bianca Venezuela Columbia Madagascar Smith."

"Bianca Venezuela Columbia Madagascar Smith, huh?" I bit the inside of my cheek to keep from laughing as I spared a glance for Landon. He looked a bit shell-shocked. "That's quite a mouthful."

"You can call me Jan."

"Jan?"

"That's my professional name," she explained. "Bianca is my stripper name. I only strip on weekends, though."

"Of course." I rolled my neck. "So, can you give a little heads-up about what's going on here?"

"Yes, and please be specific," Landon said. "Start with the part about us getting married."

"It's been on the books forever," Jan said. "You proposed during the great hotel fire last month. You were trapped in a stairwell together, running out of oxygen, and wanted to make sure that Echo knew how much you loved her. It was a glorious proposal. Everyone thought so."

"Sounds fabulous," Landon drawled. "Obviously we didn't die."

"No, you were saved by a helicopter that landed on the roof at the last minute. It was very dramatic." Jan's smile was serene. "You accidentally fell during the flight and were missing for two weeks. Your partner found you soon after, but you had amnesia. Frankly, it's a miracle you guys made it this far."

Landon shot me a rueful look. "We manage to get through everything. Go back to the amnesia, though. Are you saying I survived a fire, fell from a helicopter, got amnesia, recovered from amnesia and we're getting married all within a month?"

"Yes."

"Okay. Just asking." Landon held up his hands. "So … a wedding, huh?"

I expected him to turn tail and run, something that might occur on a sitcom rather than a soap opera. He remained where he was, though.

"I'm confused about how I can even get married," I interjected, hoping to take the onus of the conversation off Landon's broad shoulders. "I'm already married."

"Right!" Landon looked relieved when I made the point. "She's already married. She can't do it a second time."

Even though it wasn't a convenient time, I couldn't stop my agitation from bubbling up. "There's no reason to get worked up. It's not as if it's really happening."

Landon furrowed his brow. "Are you angry?"

"Should I be? It's a made-up world, Landon. You don't have to act as if I've got scales and run away to get out of whatever is going to happen here. It's not real."

"Bay … ." Landon's expression shifted into something I couldn't identify. "I didn't mean it like that."

"It doesn't matter." I shook off my irritation. "Let's just get through this." I focused on Jan. "Tell me how it is I'm not a bigamist and I'll start moving through this scene."

"You divorced Mr. Ferrigno on Witch Island six weeks ago," Jan explained. "It was in all the newspapers. You managed to get a quickie divorce even though he would've contested it if he'd known. He was unhappy, but you're free.

"You told me this story," she continued. "Why don't you remember it?"

"I suffered from a bout of amnesia earlier in the day, too," I replied. "I'm still getting over it."

Jan looked relieved. "I'm glad to hear that."

"Yes, that's the highlight of both of our days." Landon turned to me. "What do you think we're supposed to do here?"

"Follow the story."

"And that means ... getting married?" He said it with equal parts trepidation and doubt.

"It's a soap wedding," I offered. "We won't make it to the 'I dos.' Something will happen to interrupt the ceremony. You'll be safe."

"That's not what I was getting at, Bay." Landon's irritation was palpable. "I simply want to know what's about to happen. I don't think that's asking too much."

"Of course not." I tugged on my limited patience. "While you're figuring out what you want to do, I'll head to wherever it is I'm supposed to be getting ready. I'm sure there's a bridal room here."

Jan beamed. "There most definitely is. Your bridesmaids are waiting for you."

"Great." I was stiff when I turned to Landon. "I'll bet Clove and Thistle are my bridesmaids. You should go wherever Jan wants you to go, and find Sam and Marcus. I'll see you at the altar, if you're there. Don't panic. I guarantee it will be interrupted."

Landon wrapped his fingers around my wrists to still me. "I'll see you in a few minutes."

"Great." I refused to look him in the eye. "I'm looking forward to it."

"I AM GOING TO RIP that old lady's throat out with a pair of tweezers," I announced when I found Clove and Thistle standing in the middle of the bridal suite a few minutes later. They both wore pastel dresses straight out of a nightmare. "Why do you look like pieces of saltwater taffy?"

"Because apparently Aunt Tillie is a diabolical loon," Thistle replied, twirling in front of the mirror so her peach-colored dress fanned out. "I truly hate that woman."

"That's what she wants." I glanced around, the leading edge of my irritation dulling. "I suppose there's a dress I have to wear."

Clove, who seemed more at ease in her mint-colored dress, pointed toward a garment bag hanging over a dressing room door. "There."

"Is it as hideous as your dresses?"

"We haven't looked yet," Thistle replied. "We were too busy ogling the monstrosities Jan laid out for us. She's an evil woman, by the way."

"She doesn't seem that bad to me." I was resigned as I trudged forward. "I guess we should get this show on the road."

"What's wrong with you?" Thistle asked.

"Isn't it obvious? We're stuck in a soap opera world, and I've officially had my fill of it. I want to go home."

"We all feel that way," Clove offered. "You seem a lot worse off than when we saw you ten minutes ago."

"I'm fine."

"You're pretty far from fine," Thistle argued. "What's going on?"

"Yeah, spill," Clove said.

I opened my mouth to tell them exactly what was wrong and then snapped it shut. Now wasn't the time to whine and feel sorry for myself. "It doesn't matter." I vigorously shook my head. "It's nothing."

"It's something to you," Thistle countered. "Maybe you should tell us so we can hash it out."

"I'd rather just get through this." I grabbed the garment bag and yanked down the zipper, internally gagging at the mountains of white taffeta that rolled out. "Oh, this is going to be bad."

"Of course it's going to be bad," Clove said. "Aunt Tillie was the wedding designer. What did you expect?"

"I'd better get this on." I tugged the dress to free it from the bag. I would be swimming in it by the time I was dressed. "I have a feeling this is going to be a typical soap wedding, so hopefully I won't be wearing it very long."

"You mean you think it will be interrupted," Thistle surmised. "I've been wondering that, too. I hope whatever interrupts it isn't terrible … like another bear or something."

"We all hope that." I unsnapped my jeans. "I just know this dress is going to suck yeti balls."

"Well, you picked the right color if that's going to happen," Thistle said brightly. "You'll practically disappear into the landscape if that becomes an issue. Get in it. We can't make fun of you until we see it."

Oh, well, that was something to look forward to.

"I JUST CAN'T EVEN ... ."

Thistle fell to the floor ten minutes later. I knew how bad the dress looked. I got a glimpse of myself in the mirror before stepping out of the dressing room. It was even worse than I thought, if that was possible.

"Don't hold back on my account," I said dryly.

"Oh, it's not so bad." Clove's sympathetic nature was on full display as she circled me. "It's just a little ... retro."

"Retro?" Thistle laughed so hard I thought she might split a pastel seam. "She looks like a giant cotton ball ... with additional ruffles just in case we thought the miles of lace were too subtle."

I bit back a hot retort. It wasn't Thistle's fault, of course. If I wasn't agitated with Landon, I would probably be as amused as she was. Instead, my temper threatened to explode and I couldn't stop scratching the back of my neck where the lace seemed to gather together into a choker of doom and chafe the hell out of my skin.

"Knock it off," Clove warned, extending a threatening finger in Thistle's direction. "You're not helping matters."

"Oh, I didn't know I was supposed to help." Thistle was instantly contrite. "Is that what I'm supposed to be doing?"

"You don't have to do anything you don't want to do." I gathered the dress skirt and stomped toward the door. "Are you guys ready?"

"Not until you tell us what's wrong," Clove replied. "Don't deny there's something wrong. I can tell there is."

"It's not so much that there's something wrong," I hedged. "It's that ... Landon freaked out when he heard we were going to get married. He acted as if it was the scariest thing he'd ever come up against ... and he's seen poltergeists and witches now. It was a bit insulting."

"He freaked out before he saw the dress?" Thistle tilted her head to the side. "Well, he's going to run when he sees you now."

"Ha, ha."

"Leave her alone," Clove ordered. "She's upset because Landon was upset."

"Of course he's upset. He's marrying a cotton ball."

"She doesn't get it," I snapped. "It doesn't matter. This isn't real. That's exactly what I told him. It won't get to the vows anyway. Something will happen to derail it before we get to that part."

Thistle sobered. "Do you want it to get to that part?"

I shrugged. "No. I mean … I don't want this to be my real wedding. I don't want anything of the sort to happen here. I also don't want Landon to be terrified at the mere notion of a wedding, especially when it's fake."

"Oh." Realization dawned on Thistle's face. "I get why you're upset, but he's been through a lot today. I wouldn't hold this against him."

"I'm not." I honestly wasn't. "I'm just … irritated. I don't see why he had to make such a big deal about it."

"Probably because he wants you guys to do this stuff on your own timetable," Thistle explained. "It's not that he doesn't want to do this – I think he really does – but it's almost too much for him to deal with at this point in the night. It seems like we've been at this forever."

"Do you really think he wants to do it?" I felt pathetic asking the question, but I couldn't stop myself.

"I do," Thistle confirmed. "Trust me. He's not running. This probably agitates him for the same reason it agitates us."

"And that's because … ?"

"Because we're fried. We've been running around dealing with stuff we shouldn't have to deal with and we're emotionally spent. We're beyond dealing with something this big, but we have to get through it if we expect to make it home."

"And you think that's all it is?"

Thistle's gaze was pointed when she nodded. "I know that's all it is. Have a little faith. Landon isn't the type of guy to run from this. He is the type of guy to get frustrated because it's getting forced on him and he had no input."

Her words soothed me. "Yeah. He's at the end of his rope."

"Let's just hope he uses that rope on Aunt Tillie when we get back." Thistle flashed an impish smile. "Are you ready?"

I nodded. "I guess."

"Not quite," Clove countered, shuffling closer so she could plant a tiara on top of my head. She grinned when she stood back to get a better look. "Now you're ready."

"Oh, I really hate Aunt Tillie right now. She'd better start running before we wake up, because if we catch her ... ."

"We'll squash her like a bug," Thistle finished. "Come on. We have to get through this if we expect to get a chance to squash her. We've got to be near the end. There's very little else she can throw at us."

Unfortunately, I was fairly certain she jinxed us with those words. I wisely kept that to myself.

Who else wants amnesia? I think it would be totally cool to wake up with no idea who you are, who your family is – especially that part because we have Aunt Tillie – but also have a husband who looks like that. That's like my life goal now. Wait … does that make me shallow? Meh. I don't care. I'm fine being shallow.

– Clove on her favorite soap's new hunk

SIXTEEN

I heard the wedding march build to a crescendo as I followed Clove and Thistle through the church. We stopped outside the main room and glanced at one another before taking the obvious next step.

"This is kind of exciting, huh?" Clove was almost giddy. "Bay is getting married. We're bridesmaids. This is always how I pictured it happening."

I held up a ruffle on my dress's skirt. "Really? You pictured this?"

Clove shrugged, unbothered. "You might hate me for saying it, but yes. I didn't picture the ugly dresses. I pictured this moment, though."

There was something so earnest about her expression I couldn't help but smile. "I bet you pictured you doing it first."

"I am engaged," Clove agreed. "Still, you're the oldest. Part of me thinks it should've happened this way all along."

"Something tells me you won't feel the same way when something dramatic happens to implode this fake wedding."

"Oh, I'll definitely still be glad you were the first when that happens." Clove beamed. "Just think, though, we'll be able to tell this story forever and it's not even real. I'm kind of excited."

I exchanged a weighted look with Thistle. She was the snarkiest member of our little trio. Even she looked mildly touched by Clove's delight.

"Well, I'm glad you're excited." I pointed her toward the nave. "Now, I believe you're supposed to march that ugly dress down the aisle."

Clove saluted. "I'll be waiting for you on the other side."

"I know you will."

I watched her go for a moment, torn. Then I looked at Thistle. "Do you ever want to smack her over the head to get her to shut up?"

Thistle barked out a laugh. "Often."

"Me, too."

"Not today, though," she added. "Today she's right. We should enjoy this for what it is."

"And what's that?"

"A fun memory we'll never forget. This isn't real, but that doesn't mean it's entirely fake either. Just enjoy it."

"And if I turn that corner and Landon isn't at the end of the aisle?"

"He will be."

"How can you be sure?"

"Because I'm not an idiot." Thistle lamely patted my shoulder, her attempt at solace falling short. "I'm not sure about much in life. For example, I have no idea why Aunt Tillie is still alive. She's ticked off enough people that someone should have shot her in the face a long time ago. That I don't get.

"Landon, though? I've always understood him," she continued. "He's at the end of the aisle. He's here for the fake thing and he'll be there for the real thing. The fact that you're worried about it means you're being a kvetch. You need to shake it off."

I scowled, annoyed. "I'm not being a kvetch."

"Believing Landon might not be there makes you a kvetch." Thistle took a step back, never breaking eye contact. "He's there. Look inside your heart. You know he's there."

I opened my mouth to argue, but Thistle cut me off with a shake of her head.

"You're a total kvetch and you look like a moron in that dress," she said. "This is still your day. Er, it's probably going to be your five minutes. You need to enjoy it."

"Why?"

"Because we're going to laugh so hard about this the next time that we get drunk it's going to be one of our favorite memories ever."

Oddly enough, I could picture that. "Okay." I bobbed my head. "Let's do this."

"I'll be waiting for you at the end of the aisle. So will Landon. Have faith."

Thistle disappeared around the corner, leaving me alone for a few seconds to gather my thoughts. I heard the wedding march blaring in the background – the organist wasn't especially talented – and it almost drowned out my doubts. Then I thought about Landon, about his face when he smiled, and I knew Thistle was right.

I squared my shoulders and walked into the nave, my eyes instantly linking with Landon's. He stood at the end of the aisle, clad in a cheap tuxedo, and clearly fidgeting. He stopped moving the second he saw me, as if something overtook him.

I forced a smile. This was my wedding, after all, I was supposed to be happy. And, for some reason, the look on Landon's face caused me to relax.

I finished the walk down the aisle, ignoring the faces in the crowd because I didn't recognize any of them, and taking the hand Landon held out for me as he looked me up and down.

"I didn't pick the dress."

"You still look beautiful."

The catch in his breath caused me to jolt. "I think you might need glasses in this world."

"I see fine."

"The dress is a nightmare."

"I don't care."

"I'm wearing a plastic tiara."

"I don't care."

"Thistle says I'm being a kvetch."

Landon chuckled, the sound low and warm. "I don't care about that either." He lifted my hand and pressed a kiss to my palm, causing my stomach to do a little jig.

"So now you're okay with this?"

"I'm very definitely not okay with this," Landon replied. "But not for the reasons you think. It never was."

"And what are the reasons?"

"Because this is not how it's supposed to happen."

"How is it supposed to happen?"

"I don't know. I haven't planned that far ahead. This seems almost ... cruel."

I scrubbed my hand over my cheek to keep a tear or two from escaping. "It's probably going to get crueler."

"How do you figure?"

"Just wait for it."

As if on cue, the minister standing next to us began speaking. "Dearly beloved, we are gathered here today to join this man and this woman in holy matrimony."

Landon tightened his grip on my hand. "Bay, you really do look beautiful."

"And you really need glasses. I appreciate the sentiment, though."

"Here we go."

I smiled. I could do nothing else. Then I heard it, the sound that would ruin the wedding and cause Thistle to laugh herself silly for weeks. It came in the form of a motorcycle, and when I turned in slow motion – no, seriously, it was slow motion – I found a motorcycle racing up the aisle.

Michael Ferrigno, his eyes full of fury, sat astride the bike, and he looked anything but happy.

"Oh, well, I guess I should've realized he was coming back," Landon muttered. "It was too good to be true without him. If he pinches your butt, I'm totally going to slap him silly."

I snickered as I released his hand. "It will be okay." I focused on Michael. "How are things?"

"Really? That's what you want to ask me?" Michael's anger was so strong it almost knocked me over. "You divorced me!"

"I heard. That must have been ... rough ... for you."

"Rough? You pledged to love and honor me for the rest of our lives," Michael seethed. "That didn't happen. You left me."

"I'm sure you had it coming," Landon said dryly.

"No one is talking to you, turncoat!" Michael snapped. "You're the reason for all of this. You're the reason I lost her. You're the reason I lost the diamond. It's you. You did this to me." He pulled a gun from his pocket and pointed it at Landon.

I moved to slide in front of Landon, but he was having none of it.

"Don't even think about it," Landon warned.

"Landon ... ."

I jolted at the sound of the gunshot. It happened so fast ... so, so fast. I widened my eyes as I searched Landon's face, but he didn't grimace or clutch at his chest. After what felt like forever – in real time it was probably only three seconds – I turned to look at the rest of the wedding guests.

Michael had been shot. He clutched at his chest and made a big show of dying. Of course, he was playing it to the extreme – there were silent movie stars who overacted less – but when he finally went down to his knees and I recognized the fake blood swimming through his fingers, I understood that someone else had fired the shot.

"I will haunt you to your dying day," Michael rasped.

"I'm sure that will be terrible," I said, moving my eyes to the balcony that overlooked the nave. Aunt Tillie stood there, wearing a white dress that was even gaudier than the one she'd picked out for me. The gun boasted a wisp of overdramatized smoke, and her eyes were predatory.

"There she is!" Clove stated the obvious as she stomped her foot.

"There she is," Thistle agreed, her face twisting into an evil grimace. "Get her!"

WE GAVE CHASE.

What else could we do? Michael wasn't real, and even though he was clearly dragging out his death scene, it wasn't as if we cared about his fate. Aunt Tillie, on the other hand, was in control of our fates. We needed to find her – and we needed to do it now.

We opted for the back hallway of the church, figuring she would have to descend the stairs. She probably realized we were waiting, though, because she didn't do as we initially envisioned. Instead, she crouched at the top and peered around the upstairs wall, giving herself a clear view of us.

"I had no choice," Aunt Tillie announced. "I did what I had to do."

"You act as if we care about what you did to Michael," Thistle called out. "Although ... he was your son on this show. Why did you shoot him?"

"He wasn't my son. My son died long ago. His father – the devil incarnate – had his brain transplanted into Michael's body. He thought I wouldn't notice, but he had no idea who he was dealing with."

Aunt Tillie fired a shot into the ceiling, causing me to drop lower as Landon covered my head.

"Why is the brain transplant story back?" Landon complained. "That was the dumbest one."

"Really?" Thistle drawled. "I thought Chief Terry as a vampire was the top of the lame heap."

"That one was just funny." Landon knit his eyebrows as he watched me struggle with the back of my dress. "What are you doing, sweetie?"

"I need to get this off."

"Why? I already said you're beautiful in it."

"Yes, and that was a lovely sentiment. It itches, though. Kind of like I have ants in my pants."

"Oh." Landon kept one eye on the stairs as he moved behind me. "Do you have anything on under this?"

"My bra and underwear."

"And you're going to run around in that?"

"I just need this off, Landon. I'm not lying about the itching. It's starting to hurt."

"Okay. Hold on." Landon unzipped the back of the dress. It was a relief to step out of it.

Of course, because it was soap opera world and everything was surreal, I found I had a new outfit waiting for me underneath. "What the heck? I didn't put this on."

Landon took one look at the snug jeans and low-cut top and smiled. "That's kind of nice." He dipped his finger into the top and pulled it out. "Very nice."

I slapped his hand away. "We're getting toward the end of the storyline," I reminded him. "There's no way she's going to give us time for that now."

"I can wait." Landon smacked a kiss against my lips.

"Why are you suddenly in such a good mood?"

"I have no idea. It's nice, though, huh?"

"Very nice."

"Stop focusing on each other and focus on me," Aunt Tillie bellowed. "I'm the leading lady."

Landon heaved out a sigh. "You're not my leading lady."

"I can change that."

The meaning of her words hung like an icy curtain over the room, and Landon involuntarily shuddered. "I'm good."

"That's what I thought," Aunt Tillie barked. "Now, I was in the middle of confessing why I did what I did. Stop focusing on Echo's outfit and pay attention to me."

"I apologize," Landon said. "Please continue with your confession. I'm enjoying it a great deal." He took the opportunity to look down my shirt a second time. "A great, great deal."

"He had to die," Aunt Tillie repeated. Luckily she couldn't see Landon, because he was feeling a bit amorous and he opted to rub his cheek against mine rather than pay attention to whatever she was doing on the second floor. "He was evil. His father was evil, and that evil took over after the brain transplant."

"Why would you marry an evil man?" Clove asked.

"He tricked me."

"Really, the great and omnipotent Alexis Kane was tricked. I'm shocked." Thistle made an exaggerated face. "By the way, why do you have a different name than your kid?"

"Because I didn't take any of my husbands' names. Why is that important?"

"Husbands? As in plural?" Landon moved his mouth from my neck. "How many times were you married?"

"Fourteen, and I made a lovely bride each and every time."

Landon's eyebrows flew up his forehead. "Fourteen? You found fourteen men dumb enough to marry you?"

"I can see I should've shot you when I ended Michael's torment," Aunt Tillie growled. "You've got a mouth on you."

"I think that's rich coming from you. Still, I'm willing to forgive everything you've done if you come down here right now and send us home."

Aunt Tillie didn't immediately answer, so I stuck my head around the end of the stairwell in the hope I'd catch a glimpse of her. She'd positioned herself so she was in the exact right spot to catch my gaze.

"Hello, Echo."

"I have to hand it to you, Aunt Tillie, you're going all out with this one." I worked overtime to keep my tone even. "You're staying in character. You've created an elaborate storyline. Everything is coming together for us, isn't it?"

"I have no idea what you're talking about."

"How much longer?"

"I have no idea." Aunt Tillie's grin was impish. "Admit it. You're having fun, aren't you?"

"I wouldn't call it fun."

"How can you not find this enjoyable? It's exhilarating."

"It's fun for you. It's harder for us."

"How can you say that? Look at everything you've gotten to do today. You even got married."

"Not really." I swallowed hard. "That was almost painful."

"No, it wasn't." Aunt Tillie's eyes sparkled. "It was cathartic for you because you weren't sure Landon would be there when you turned that corner. But he was there, and that erased any and all doubts you've ever had. It bolstered you."

"Landon?" I raised an eyebrow. "I thought his name was Jericho. You just showed your hand, Aunt Tillie. I wasn't sure until this exact moment if you were real or simply an image you inserted into the storyline. Now I know."

"You think you know," Aunt Tillie corrected. "You don't know anything yet."

"I know there's only one way out of here, and we're not going to allow you to escape."

Aunt Tillie snorted. "I created this world, Bay. Do you really think I don't have an exit plan?" She winked before disappearing behind the wall. When she spoke again, her voice was much farther away. "I always have an exit plan."

"Crap." Landon didn't hesitate before bolting up the stairs.

I followed, scanning the empty balcony before fixing my eyes on the door at the far side of the space. It was ajar. Aunt Tillie had clearly escaped through it.

"I really should've seen that coming," I lamented.

"Yeah, well, let's go." Landon held out his hand. "We have to be getting close to the end. What else could she possibly do?"

That was a scary thought.

So she somehow fell under mind control, turned into a serial killer, got possessed by the Devil and is still considered the show's heroine? Where can I sign up for that gig? I've got a few ideas.

– Aunt Tillie on how to be the perfect heroine

SEVENTEEN

We hit the door that led outside, finding ourselves in another wooded environment. Because it looked as if we would have to start hoofing it, Clove and Thistle stripped out of their terrible bridesmaids' dresses and found impractical soap outfits underneath.

"I would be better off going barefoot than wearing these shoes," Thistle groused as she glared at her heels. "It's not as if I'll be able to run in them."

"Aunt Tillie is old," Clove pointed out. "How fast can she run?"

That was a question I couldn't answer. "It's her world. She knows all the tricks."

"And she wants us to follow," Landon said. "The thing is, she doesn't want us to catch her ... yet."

"So what do we do?" Thistle was at her limit as she lifted a shoe to stare at the icepick heel. "These shoes are all kinds of stupid."

"At least you're not wearing a shirt that completely shows off your assets," I noted, pointing to my chest.

"Oh, we're going to see if we can keep that shirt." Landon grinned. "I'm a big fan."

"Maybe they'll have it in the gift shop."

"We can only hope."

"I think my shirt is worse," Clove complained, stepping to the center of our little circle so she could show off her impressive cleavage. "It's so tight I can barely breathe. I don't think it's very flattering either."

"I think it's flattering." It was. Clove was the most well-endowed of all of us, and her assets were clearly on display thanks to Aunt Tillie's new wardrobe. "In fact, I think you look nice."

Clove wasn't convinced. "What do you think, Sam?"

"Hmm." Sam jerked his eyes from Clove's cleavage. "Did you say something, honey?"

Marcus snorted. "I think we know how Sam feels."

"Do you think it's indecent, Landon?" Clove asked, her eyes wide with worry. "I don't want to make a name for myself. Aunt Tillie always told me that was a possibility if I wore the wrong clothes."

I scowled. "She never should've told you that."

"Yeah, from the woman who wears leggings that show off ... well, everything. I wouldn't take her fashion advice to heart," Thistle said. "But I want to know why you two got slutty shirts and I got one that covers everything."

"It's because you don't have anything to show off." Landon clearly responded before he thought better of it. "I mean ... um ... Bay, I think this one is for you to answer."

I shot him a withering look. "Really? After you've screwed it up you want me to swoop in and smooth things over? Why isn't that surprising?"

"Hey, I'm doing the best I can." Landon wagged a finger in my face. "I'm still traumatized from the wedding that never was."

I made a face, although it didn't last because his expression was far too charming. "You're incorrigible sometimes."

"That's why you love me." Landon looked back to Thistle. "I shouldn't have said that. I'm sure you have plenty to show off. I'm not looking, mind you, but I'm sure you do."

Thistle rolled her eyes and made a "well, duh" face. "Don't push it. I can only take so much in one day."

"Join the club." Landon grabbed my hand. "We have to follow the trail Aunt Tillie is bound to leave. She wants to lead us to a final destination. I think we can all agree on that. It was the same in the fairy tale world. I don't think this will be any different."

"So we just wander into the woods?" Thistle gestured toward the fake woodland setting. "What if there's another bear in there? What if there's something worse?"

"We've already dealt with butt-pinching mobsters, lame vampires and a dude who fell into a crack in the floor at the hospital. How much worse can it get?"

"Ugh." Thistle, Clove and I groaned in unison.

"What?" Landon held his hands out, clueless. "What did I say?"

"You totally jinxed us, man," Marcus complained. "Now something really terrible will happen. Just you watch."

"Yeah, yeah." Landon waved off the comment and moved toward the clearly-marked path through the trees. There was even a sign that said "This way" with a pointing arrow to make sure we didn't fall victim to idiocy. "I'm getting hungry. Do you think there's bacon in this world?"

Of course he would ask that. "Do you really want to try eating it given the fact that Aunt Tillie's aware of your fondness for pork? I can guarantee you'd be safer eating the asparagus in this world."

"Are those my only two options?"

"I don't see where you have any options. We're in the woods. You're not going to find food here."

"Fine. But when we get out of here I'm going to eat enough bacon to make it through the rest of winter."

"Duly noted."

"WHAT THE HECK IS this?"

We'd only been walking for five minutes when we came across a wishing well in the middle of the forest. Sam was the first to approach, wrinkling his nose as he circled the contraption.

"I think this is papier mâché, too," he offered. "Why would someone put a papier mâché well in the middle of the woods?"

That was a good question. Unfortunately, I had an idea what the answer would be. "Look inside," I prodded.

Sam snagged gazes with me. "Why? What's inside? I'm not going to find a body in there or anything, am I?"

I shook my head. "No. Although I'll bet it's not empty."

"I have no idea what that means," Sam whined. "I just know I don't want to look now. Someone else should look. Clove, I think this is a job for you."

"Oh, really?" Clove made a face. "Aren't you supposed to protect me? We are getting married, after all. You're the man. You're supposed to be my protector."

"You'd better hope Aunt Tillie didn't hear you say that," Thistle warned. "If she did, you're going to be in big trouble. She won't like that one bit."

Clove balked. "What did I say?"

"She raised us to save ourselves," I reminded her. "That was the whole point of the fairytale world. She didn't want us to rely on a man to save us when we were capable of doing it ourselves."

"So?" Clove planted her hands on her hips. "Maybe I don't want to save myself. Did you ever consider that?"

"Only every day since I've met you," I replied. "I get it. You like to be a girly girl. There's nothing wrong with that. Aunt Tillie is another story. She won't like it if you turn girly all of a sudden."

"Really?" Clove's tone was dry as she gestured toward her overflowing breasts, which were still on display. "I think she wants the world to know I'm a girl. Why else would she have given me this outfit?"

"Now isn't the time for this," Landon interjected, waving a hand between us to make sure we didn't start throwing punches. "We're clearly here for a reason. You guys think the reason is in that well. I'm a little terrified to look, but since I'm the FBI agent I'll do it."

Landon puffed out his chest. His words were bolder than his actions, because he didn't move an inch from the spot where he stood.

"I really don't want to look in there," Landon said after a beat. "I'm afraid it's going to be something freaky."

"This whole world is freaky," I reminded him. "You should be used to it by now."

"Right." Landon's shoulders were stiff when he turned back to the well. "I'll give you a hundred bucks if you look for me."

I cocked an eyebrow. "You're trying to bribe me?"

"I know I should be embarrassed, but I'm terrified to look in that well."

"I'm not above a bribe. I just want something better than a hundred bucks."

Landon tugged on his bottom lip as he turned back to me. "What do you want?"

"An hour-long massage, dinner in Traverse City and a night of just you and me."

Landon smiled. "You can have that no matter what. It's not a bribe if I already want to do it."

"Oh." I deflated a bit. "I want you to get a pedicure with me, too."

"Now you're talking." Landon bobbed his head. "Fine. But no photos this time. Last time you blasted our salon visit all over Facebook. The guys at the office are still talking about it."

"Done."

"Great." Landon took my extended hand and shook it while giving me a quick kiss. It wasn't until I was already moving that I realized he was pushing me toward the wishing well. "If it's something dangerous, yell and I'll come running. If it's merely gross, you're on your own."

"Oh, what big, strong men we have," Thistle drawled, following me toward the well.

"Aren't you afraid?" Marcus called out to her.

"No. I know what we're going to find."

"How do you know?"

"Because wells on soaps are a tried and true story," I answered for Thistle. "They've been used multiple times. I think we all know what's in here."

"And what's that?"

"An evil twin," Thistle and I answered in unison, shuffling toward the lip of the well and looking down. Sure enough, sitting in the center of the papier mâché well – a structure she could break out of whenever she wanted – sat one of Aunt Tillie's clones. I knew it wasn't the real Aunt Tillie, because the woman was dressed in dowdy clothes and had fake grime spread from one end of her face to the other.

"How's it going in there?" I asked, doing my best not to smile. Even though it was a fake environment, it shouldn't have been funny. Being trapped in a well is never funny.

"Thank the Goddess you're here." The woman scrambled to her feet, which conveniently put her about a foot away from us. All she had to do was raise her arms and we could've lifted her out. Neither Thistle nor I made as if we intended to do that. "You have to get me out."

"How long have you been in here?" Thistle asked, looking around. "It looks a little bleak, yet completely sanitary. What's that about?"

The Aunt Tillie triplet furrowed her brow. "I have no idea what you're talking about."

"Which one are you?" I asked.

"Nikki Forrester."

"Ah, the more evil triplet." I flicked my eyes to Thistle. "I'm guessing that the most evil triplet did this. It's the only thing that makes sense from a narrative perspective."

"Who are you talking to?" Landon asked, moving to my side. "And what are you talking about?" His eyes went wide when he caught sight of the woman in the well. "Hah! We've got you. What are you going to do now?"

He was a little too triumphant for my taste. I knew that would deflate fast enough, though. "That's not Aunt Tillie. That's one of the triplets we saw at the cabin."

"The more evil one," Thistle supplied. "The most evil one is still out there."

"Oh, man." Landon pressed the heel of his hand to his forehead. "I thought we were finally getting somewhere."

"We are. We just have to figure out Aunt Tillie's endgame. If she's dusting off triplets, that means they'll play into the finale."

"And you're convinced we're close to the finale?"

Landon looked so hopeful I couldn't deny him. "I do. I think we're closer than we realize. I think we simply need to find Aunt Tillie, get through the final scene, and then she'll send us home."

"Is that something you know or something you feel?"

I shrugged. "A little of both."

"I'll take it." Landon rubbed his hand over my back as he stared at the woman in the well. "So, are we supposed to get her out of there or leave her? I could go either way on this one."

I snickered. "I think we're supposed to get her out, but first we need to come to an understanding." I leveled my gaze on Nikki. She seemed agitated. I was fine with that. In fact, I preferred it. "If we get you out of there, you have to help us catch Aunt Tillie."

"I don't know who that is." Nikki was stubborn as she folded her arms across her chest. "I've never heard that name before."

"Alexis Kane," I corrected, internally chastising myself. Aunt Tillie wanted us to play the game. If we expected to get out of here soon, we'd have to follow the rules. "We know what she's planning. In fact ... we know about the snow sharks."

Nikki rubbed her hands together, gleeful. "It's going to be glorious. We're going to bring the world to its knees so the people will worship us."

"That was a little over the top," Landon lamented. "We know about her plan. We're going to stop her ... with or without your help."

I put my hand on his arm to still him before he said something else we couldn't back up. "I have a feeling we're going to need her help."

Landon frowned. "Do you have to ruin all of my fun? I get to have so little fun in this world. Basically I've gotten to almost marry you and that's it."

I couldn't help being surprised. "You thought that was the most fun part?"

"You didn't?"

"I kind of liked the disco ball room and the power ballad," I admitted.

"We agreed never to speak of that again."

"No, you agreed never to speak of that again," I corrected. "I think I'll have some nice dreams about it."

"That's the difference between men and women," Landon complained. "You were happy with the buildup, while I wanted the happy ending."

"Is that why you liked the wedding?" It was a bold question, but I asked it all the same.

Landon nodded without hesitation. "Yes."

"Wow! And here I thought you wouldn't be waiting for me at the end of the aisle. I don't even know what to make of it. I guess I like it. Okay, I've changed my mind. That was my favorite part, too."

Landon grinned. "This is a crappy honeymoon for us, though. I would rather do it with a massage, dinner and private time."

"And a pedicure," I reminded him.

"Don't remind me." Landon turned his full attention back to Nikki. "Okay, here's the deal, we'll get you out of the well if you agree to help us take down Alexis Kane. That's your only option. If you don't agree to our terms, you're on your own."

Nikki's mouth dropped open. "You'd leave me here to suffer and die? What kind of person does that?"

"You should know," I replied. "Who shoved you in this well?"

"I ... ." Nikki broke off, thoughtful.

"It was the most evil triplet, right? Yeah, that's what I figured. We're going to have to take her on next. Once we get through with her that leaves Aunt Tillie. She'll be the last obstacle."

"How can you be sure?" Landon asked. "How do you know the most evil triplet won't be the one we face off with in the end?"

"Because true evil never makes it to the end on a soap opera," I replied. "It's the conflicted characters, the ones who aren't one thing or the other, who make it to the end. They live on in soap opera infamy."

"They're also Aunt Tillie's favorites," Thistle added. "Bay is right.

We need to form a pact with this one to take out the bad one. That leaves us with a clear shot at Aunt Tillie."

"Okay." Landon was amenable to letting us take charge. "I just have one question."

"Shoot."

"Are we actually going to see snow sharks before the end of this thing? If so, I kind of want to find an athletic cup or something."

I pursed my lips to keep from laughing. "I have no idea. I guess we'll have to find out together."

"That's the way I like discovering everything." His smile was heartfelt. "Here we go again, huh?"

"Yeah, here we go again."

I want to give birth on a soap opera. The women don't sweat, grunt only twice and their makeup doesn't even run. That's the way to do it.
– Clove on the joys of soap opera motherhood

EIGHTEEN

Nikki was not a happy triplet. Landon easily managed to tug her out of the well, and when she was on the ground next to us I got the distinct impression that she was considering running. Landon must have, too, because he grabbed her arm and shook his head before she could work up the gumption to make a break for it.

"If I have to chase you, you won't like it."

Nikki scowled. "I don't like you."

"The feeling is mutual." Landon shifted his gaze to me. "Okay. What do we do next?"

I had no idea. "Well ... we need to make a plan to catch her. To do that, we need information on where she is and exactly what she's doing."

"Okay." Landon hunkered down so he was on an even level with Nikki. "Where is she?"

"It is not my place to tell."

"Well, you have to tell me."

"No."

Landon looked to me for help. "Do you want to say anything here?"

"What do you want me to say?" I challenged. "You're the FBI agent. Isn't it your job to negotiate with terrorists?"

"Am I supposed to treat her like a terrorist?"

I shrugged. "What would you do if she was a terrorist?"

"Well, I'd slap her around and start breaking fingers." Landon winked to let me know he was kidding. I didn't have the heart to tell him that I knew all too well that he didn't have it in him to hit an old woman – even if she was a fake character in a soap opera and he was clearly tired and ready to escape.

"How else?" I asked, legitimately curious.

"I'd threaten her with jail, perhaps lock her in a federal prison until it loosened her lips. I don't think I have that option here."

He wasn't wrong. I rolled my neck and stared at the sky a moment. "We could try to curse her."

Thistle, who stood about ten feet away with Marcus, perked up at the suggestion. "Do you think we can do that here?"

"I don't know. It's worth a shot."

"Okay." Thistle flexed her fingers. "I suggest we start with the urinary tract infection spell and then tilt it into the nails on a chalkboard chant. That's always a crowd pleaser."

I watched Nikki's eyes for signs of recognition, but she didn't so much as bat an eyelash.

"It won't work on her," I announced, drawing multiple sets of eyes to me. "She's not real."

"How can you be sure?" Landon asked.

"And even if you are sure, why don't we test the curses anyway?" Thistle suggested.

I ignored her evil smile. "She's just an empty vessel. It's kind of like she's a character in a computer game. She can only do what she's programmed to do. She's not Aunt Tillie. The woman at the church was Aunt Tillie."

"I'm not doubting you," Landon said, "but how can you be absolutely sure?"

"Because the Aunt Tillie at the church didn't have to stick to a script," I replied. "She could say and do what she wanted. She knew I was upset about the wedding, that I felt it was a bit cruel. She wanted to make sure I knew why she did it."

"And why was that?"

"Because she knew that no matter how much I love and trust you, there was a part of me that worried you wouldn't be there when I turned that corner." I saw no reason to lie. "The biggest part of my heart knew you'd be there, and yet there was this little shard that started poking my innards when I saw your reaction to finding out she expected us to pretend to get married."

"Bay, I reacted that way because I thought it was cruel and mean for both of us," Landon explained. "It's not that I don't want to ... ." He broke off.

"I know it was mean." I softened my voice. "I don't think she meant for it to be mean, though. It was supposed to be an exercise in acceptance."

"I understand that, but it was still mean." Landon pushed himself to a standing position, ignoring the way Nikki glared after him. "I don't like it when she messes with us on stuff like this. I want to be able to choose our own course and not let her push us. I think that's fair."

I squeezed his hand. "It's more than fair. But that exercise was for me, not you. I'm sorry you got caught up in it."

"You think I don't get it, but I do." Landon lowered his voice as he leaned closer. "You're working hard not to worry about me disappearing. You're almost there. Aunt Tillie wanted to push you over the edge."

He understood more than I ever gave him credit for. I was always amazed when he figured things out, as if he could see directly inside my soul.

"It was still a little mean," Landon said. "But I get it. As for the other thing ... I'm always going to be there."

"I know." I smiled. "I think I've known since the moment you came back, although I didn't want to allow myself to believe it."

"Oh, will someone please gag me?" Nikki complained. "I can't watch one more second of this tripe."

"Join the club," Thistle said dryly. "Can you two stop stroking each other and focus on the bigger picture? We need this Aunt Tillie to take us to the other Aunt Tillie so we can take down the main Aunt Tillie. That won't happen if we keep hanging out here."

"Did you follow that logic?" Landon asked.

I nodded. "Sadly, I did. She's right. We have to find the other Aunt Tillie. The most evil one."

"What will you do when you find her?" Nikki asked.

"What do you want us to do?"

"Make her pay for putting me in the well."

"We can do that." I tilted my head to the side. "We need you to tell us where they are if you expect us to help you get your revenge."

Nikki blew out a sigh. "Fine. I'll tell you. In fact, I'll do better than that. I'll show you."

And just like that, I knew we were back on track. "Then let's do it."

NIKKI LED US THROUGH the woods, sticking close to the path as she cast the occasional derogatory look in my direction. I finally couldn't take her cold silence any longer, so I decided to engage with her.

"What do you know about me?"

"You were married to my nephew until you divorced him for that one." She jerked her thumb in Landon's direction. "My nephew was a complete and total psychopath. He impregnated women and threw bar glasses across the room for sport. All he had going for him was a nice set of dimples."

"I didn't really know him very well. I can't comment on his character."

"You were married to him."

"It's difficult to explain."

"Well, I knew him," Nikki said. "He was a pus-filled little jerkwad. I always hated him."

"Even before the brain transplant?"

"He was worse before the brain transplant."

"Well, I guess I'm glad I didn't know him then."

"Yeah, he was a real piece of work." Nikki leaned closer. "But he was nowhere near the douche that guy is."

I knew she was talking about Landon. The jab should've upset me, but it didn't. I figured she was merely spouting the script Aunt Tillie wrote for her. "I guess, from your point of view, that's probably true."

"What about from your point of view?"

"He's a hero. He's my hero."

Nikki smirked. "I guess there are two sides to everything?"

"I guess so."

The rest of the trip took only five minutes. By the time we hit a cabin – one that wasn't much different from the one we were at previously – I started to get a feeling for what we were up against. The landscape, which had been lush and full of color only moments before, was now covered with a powdery substance that couldn't exactly be described as snow.

"What is this?" Landon leaned over and ran his fingers through the substance. "It's not even wet. It's like … laundry detergent flakes or something. In fact … ." He lifted his fingers to his nose and sniffed. "It smells like laundry detergent."

"And it's not cold," Thistle noted, lifting her head to the sky. "It feels exactly the same as it did before, only there's snow."

"Where else would Aunt Tillie hole up to make snow sharks?" I asked.

Landon dropped the fake snow on the ground and made a face. "Are sharks going to hop up out of this stuff and try to eat us?"

"That might be fun," Thistle said, staring into the white fluff. "At least this stupid story would go out with a bang."

"Do you think this is it?" Marcus was hopeful. "Is this the end?"

I nodded. "This is the big finale. What else has she been building toward if not this?"

"Then let's get this done." Marcus was more determined than I'd ever seen him. "I'm so ready to get home."

"You realize we're probably still going to wake up with hangovers, right?" Thistle prodded.

"I don't care." Marcus was firm. "A hangover is better than this. I'm ready to be done."

"Then let's be done," a woman announced as she strolled out of the bushes to our right. Because they were barren and provided minimal cover, I had trouble believing she'd been there the entire time. Of course, that hardly mattered now.

When she turned, when her gaze landed on me and then Landon, I realized we weren't quite yet done with the drama.

"Oh, crap!" I made a face as I shook my head. "Why are you back?"

Eden offered me a chilly smile before her expression warmed and she focused on Landon. "It's been a long time, Jericho."

"It has," Landon agreed. "It's been, like, three hours."

"It's been three years," Eden corrected, her temper flashing. "I mean ... I spent one year locked in a cave with a mountain man who turned out to have a heart of gold before he died, another year working as a waitress on an island after a bout of amnesia and then another full year dealing with the aftermath of my return from the dead.

"Speaking of that, shouldn't you be surprised to see me?" she continued. "The last time we interacted was the day before I fell from a bridge and it was assumed I'd died in the water below. It should've been a traumatic experience for you."

"Oh, right." Landon slid me a sidelong look before making the universal "she's loopy" sign and twirling his finger close to his ear. "I was totally gutted about that. I felt terrible about your death."

"Yes, and this is supposed to be our big reunion," Eden said. "You're supposed to take one look at me, fall to your knees, burst into tears and propose."

Landon raised an eyebrow. "And who told you that?"

"Um ... the script." Eden made a face. "The only reason I came back was to make sure I was billed as the leading lady. Geez."

"Aunt Tillie's world is starting to fall apart," I noted. "This happened in the fairytale world, too. The actors became real and the bleeding was pronounced at the end."

"That's music to my ears," Landon said. "But we still have to get through this scene. We still have to get our hands on Aunt Tillie."

"Why do you think I'm here?" Eden asked. "I'm the one who is going to catch her."

"In a weird way it makes sense," Clove offered. "She was one of the first people we saw. We've come full circle. Now she's here at the end."

"Let's hope this really is the end," Sam said. "I can't take much more of this."

"None of us can," Landon said. "Trust me. The last thing I wanted to see was this crazy chick." He gestured toward Eden. "But we're here. If we work together, we'll get home. We need to believe in that and refrain from fighting from here on out."

"That sounds like absolutely no fun," Thistle complained. "In fact ... ." She didn't get a chance to finish what she was saying because Eden picked that moment to lash out and smack Landon across the face.

He wasn't expecting it, so he rocked back on his heels, instinctively reaching up to touch the spot where she'd struck him. "What the ... ?"

"That's for moving on when you should've been pining for me," Eden announced.

"Yeah, I'm done here." Landon's frustration was so strong it practically slapped me across the face. "We need to end this."

"I think you're going to get your wish," Nikki said, lifting her hand and pointing toward the cabin. "There she is."

I jerked my gaze to where she pointed, my heart leaping at the sight of Aunt Tillie. She stood in a slinky black gown and held what looked to be a large diamond in her hand. She smiled as she scanned faces, evil delight flitting through her eyes.

"I see you've come to stop me," she announced. "I won't go quietly."

"Oh, we don't want you to go quietly," Thistle snapped. "We want you to scream, yell and cry." She moved toward Aunt Tillie. "We want you to beg."

"Then come and get me." Aunt Tillie turned and ran, showing a bolt of speed that shouldn't have been possible given her age.

Thistle moved to give chase, along with Eden, who was quick to follow, but I grabbed Thistle's arm and held her back.

"What are you doing?" Thistle sputtered. "We have to catch her."

"That's not her."

"Yes, it is. You saw her. She had the diamond."

"That's not her." I looked to Nikki for confirmation. "That's Marlena Bauer. That's the most evil corner of the triangle."

"How can you be sure?" Landon asked.

"Because that's Aunt Tillie." I inclined my chin to the front door, to where the Aunt Tillie we recognized from the real world stepped through the door. She wore camouflage pants, a combat helmet and carried what looked to be a ray gun of some sort.

"That is her," Landon said, pursing his lips. "She used the other woman as a decoy."

"So what do we do?" Clove asked. "I mean ... do we chase her?"

"That's not necessary," Thistle announced, putting her head down as she headed in Aunt Tillie's direction. "I've got this."

"Wait!"

It was too late. Thistle was determined. She wasn't about to give up until she had Aunt Tillie in her clutches.

"Should we follow?" Landon asked, deferring to me.

I had no idea how. "I guess so. I mean ... I don't know what else to do."

So that's what we did. We chased after Aunt Tillie, who made a big show of running around the cabin while trying not to get too far ahead or make any sudden moves that might allow her to escape. She didn't drop the ray gun until Thistle launched herself at Aunt Tillie's diminutive form.

The two bodies hit with a loud thud. Aunt Tillie was solid, but Thistle was fueled by ultimate rage. Aunt Tillie conveniently landed in a huge pile of snow. Thankfully there was no shark to go with it. When she hit, her breath was knocked out of her lungs and Thistle had an easy time rolling her onto her back.

Thistle straddled Aunt Tillie, holding her arms to the ground and slamming her butt down to keep Aunt Tillie pinned every time our elderly great-aunt tried to buck her.

"Knock it off!" Thistle ordered, her tone authoritative. "It's time to go home."

Aunt Tillie snorted. She didn't look particularly perturbed about being caught. "Not yet."

"It's time," Thistle said. "We're done. We don't want to stay."

"The story isn't done yet," Aunt Tillie argued.

"We caught you before you made snow sharks a reality," Thistle challenged. "The story is done."

"Of course it's not."

"But ... ." Thistle was helpless when she turned to me. "You said this was the end."

Apparently I'd miscalculated. "What else is there left to do?"

"Why, I have to face trial, of course." Aunt Tillie beamed. "I need my day in court."

Oh, well, crap! I definitely should've seen that coming. If there's one thing Aunt Tillie loves more than soaps, it's old *Matlock* episodes.

"Is she saying what I think she's saying?" Landon asked.

I nodded, my stomach twisting.

"Well, that's just great." Landon glared at Aunt Tillie. "I hope you know you're on my list."

"I'm looking forward to seeing what you do with that, Sparky." Aunt Tillie happily wiggled her hips. "I can't wait to get on the witness stand. It'll be epic."

Something told me it was going to be something other than epic.

This show keeps making a big deal about multiple personalities, but I feel like I have them every month during PMS. It's not a big deal. Take some Midol and grab a heating pad, and you'll be fine in three hours.

– Bay on soap opera mental health

NINETEEN

"I'm so tired."

The trip the courthouse was short. The soap opera authorities – who looked as if they couldn't keep a cardboard box safe, let alone contain Aunt Tillie – collected her by the door and whisked her to whatever holding cell they kept in the back. She shot me a triumphant look as she walked away, as if this was always what she wanted.

That made me inexplicably nervous.

"Come here." Landon sat on a courtroom bench and lifted his arm so I could skirt underneath it. "What hurts?"

The question caught me off guard. "Is something supposed to hurt?"

"I mean your neck and shoulders."

"Oh. My shoulders. This doesn't count as part of the massage you owe me."

"Of course not." Landon dug his fingers into the sore spot between my shoulder blades, eliciting a moan for his efforts. "See, why would I want to cut down on that noise in the future?"

I offered up a rueful look. "You're kind of a pervert."

"I'm just trying to look forward to finally getting out of here."

"I'm sorry about that."

"Sorry about what?"

"I thought the scene at the cottage was the end. Apparently I was wrong."

"Yeah, well, you can't be right all of the time." Landon pressed a kiss to the back of my head and then continued rubbing. "What do you think she's going to do now?"

"I think she wants to get on the witness stand and do a Jack Nicholson."

Landon furrowed his brow. "You mean from *A Few Good Men*?"

"Pretty much. She's always loved that scene. This is her chance to do her version of it."

"That's a terrifying thought." Landon rolled his neck until it cracked. "Do you think that will be the end?"

"I hope so."

"But do you think it will be?"

"I thought the cabin would be the end, so what do I know?"

Landon heaved out a sigh and pulled me in for a hug. "We're close. It won't be long now. I can feel it."

"Yeah, I'm almost looking forward to the hangover I'm going to have when I wake up."

"I'll tell you one thing, I've learned my lesson about drinking in a house with that woman," Landon said. "From now on when we get rip-roaring drunk and decide to dance, it's going to be under our own roof. Oh, and we'll be naked when it happens."

I might've been exhausted, but I was genuinely amused at the way his mind worked. "Good plan."

"Thank you."

We lapsed into comfortable silence, Marcus and Thistle paired off to the left and Clove and Sam to the right. As if tied together, we jerked our heads to the back of the courtroom at the sound of footsteps. I could only sigh when I saw the well-dressed woman in the smart business suit heading in our direction.

"This is definitely the end," Thistle noted when she caught sight of the woman. "She's cast Aunt Willa in this one. There must be a reason."

"She's Aunt Tillie's ultimate enemy," I agreed. "I'm guessing she's the prosecuting attorney. It only makes sense that it would be Aunt Willa pushing her on the stand when she gets her big moment."

"Oh, well, this might be fun." Landon gave Aunt Willa a pinched smile. "How are you, ma'am?"

"The name is Ima Doodyhead," Aunt Willa barked. "I'll be the one making sure that Alexis Kane finally pays for the damage she's done to this world."

I tried to keep a straight face. No, really I did. The second my gaze snagged with Thistle's, though, we burst into hysterical laughter.

"Ima Doodyhead? That's probably the best name I've heard since I got to this place." I felt Landon's shoulders shaking with silent laughter as he tugged me back against him. "Well, Ms. Doodyhead, how can we be of assistance?"

"You'll all be taking the stand," she replied. "We need your testimony to make sure that Alexis doesn't manage to walk away ... again."

"Just out of curiosity, how many times has she been on trial?" Landon asked.

"Thirty-six."

"Of course." Landon pressed the heel of his hand to his forehead. "What do you want us to do?"

"I merely want you to tell the truth when it's your turn on the stand."

"And that's it?"

"That's it."

Landon exchanged a weighted look with me before nodding in capitulation. "Okay then. Let's start testifying."

SAM WAS UP FIRST.

It made sense. Aunt Tillie wanted to build tension, so that meant she was saving those of us she really wanted to torture until the end. I knew I'd be one of the last to go. I figured Thistle might be the ultimate witness. There was a good chance it might be Landon, too. I wasn't sure which outcome would serve us better.

As for Sam, he looked so tired I almost felt sorry for him.

"What can you tell us about your interaction with Ms. Kane?" Aunt Willa asked, pacing the floor between Sam and Aunt Tillie. Aunt Tillie sat in a huge reclining chair behind the defense table, what looked to be an entire team of high-priced lawyers helping her along, and she appeared more amused than worried.

"I have no idea," Sam answered. "You need to be more specific."

"Okay, more specifically, what did you see at the cabin when you went with your friends to apprehend Ms. Kane?"

"Oh, well, her more evil triplet led us to the cabin and then magically disappeared at the same time her most evil triplet took off in the woods. Then she walked out of the cabin with a ray gun and Thistle tackled her. Then we miraculously ended up here."

"And who is Thistle?"

"Oh, right." Sam searched his memory. "Cora Devane. She tackled Ms. Kane."

Aunt Willa smiled. "Thank you. No further questions."

"That's it?" Sam moved to stand, but a member of Aunt Tillie's dream team held up a hand to still him. "That's not all. I should've known."

"I have just one question." The man had broad shoulders and a bushy beard, sparkplug eyebrows and a smarmy smile. I disliked him on sight. "I'm Reginald Winthrop Warren Windbag Jr.," he introduced himself. "I'm lead counsel for Ms. Kane."

"Your name is Windbag?" Sam smiled. "That's just ... awesome."

Reginald ignored the dig. "As I said, I have only one question for you."

"Great."

"How long have you hated the defendant?"

Whatever question Sam was expecting, that clearly wasn't it. "I don't hate her."

"Do you like her?"

"Not right now."

"So how long have you hated her?"

Sam shrugged. "About three hours."

"No more questions, your honor."

"You may take your seat, Mr. Wharton."

The judge spoke for the first time, and I couldn't help smiling when I recognized Chief Terry. He looked grave, a gavel gripped in his hand as if he were really listening, and I found the entire scene adorable.

"He's a vampire by night and a judge by day," I mused. "That's kind of fun."

"Yes, I can't wait to tell him about it." Landon tightened his grip on my hand. "One down. Five to go."

"Six to go," I corrected. "Aunt Tillie has to take the stand, too. She'll be the finale."

"I can't wait for that."

MARCUS' QUESTIONS WERE EVEN sparser than the ones hurled at Sam.

"How is it that you grew to be so handsome?" Aunt Willa asked.

"Just lucky, I guess."

"No further questions, your honor."

"I have no questions for this witness," Reginald said.

Thistle made a disgusted face. "I always knew he was her favorite. She's not even torturing him a little bit."

"You sound disappointed about that," Landon said dryly.

"It's not fair."

"Life isn't fair," I supplied. "Didn't Aunt Tillie always tell us that?"

Thistle wasn't about to be appeased. "I'm totally going to choke that old woman to death when we get home. I'm not kidding. I'm really going to do it this time."

We both knew it wasn't true, but it was a nice thought.

CLOVE WAS A BUNDLE OF nerves when it was her turn. She

squirmed as she tried to get comfortable on the witness stand. Aunt Willa's stance was much more aggressive when she approached.

"Ms. Cramer, what can you tell us about your interaction with the accused?"

"Not much," Clove replied. "She's been mean and weird ... and she stole a diamond. I'm not even sure I understand most of this world. I think you should ask someone else, because I don't like being up here."

"You have to answer the questions being posed," Chief Terry ordered. "That's your responsibility as a witness."

"I don't like it when people stare at me," Clove shot back.

"Well, that's too bad." Chief Terry was firm. "You must testify. If you don't, I'll hold you in contempt of court."

Clove did exactly as I expected and burst into tears. They weren't real, of course. She could've been a soap opera actress, given her propensity for manipulating emotions. She'd been perfecting the art of crying on cue since we were kids. She'd gotten quite good at it.

"Why on earth are you crying?" Aunt Willa complained.

"I'm not crying." Clove swiped at her cheeks. "My eyes are leaking."

"That's not going to get you out of answering questions."

Clove looked to Chief Terry to see if that was true. In typical fashion, he folded like a shirt on a clothing store display rack at the sight of her tears.

"She's done," Chief Terry announced.

"I'm not done with her," Aunt Willa argued.

"And I haven't even had a chance to talk to her," Reginald challenged.

"And yet she's still done." Chief Terry was firm. "Witness dismissed."

Clove kept her back to Chief Terry as she walked toward us. She looked smugger than Aunt Tillie. "I guess I handled that, huh?"

I guess she did.

TO MY SURPRISE, THISTLE was called next. She was absolutely furious when she realized what was happening.

"I knew it!" She stomped her foot as she stood.

"You knew what?" Landon asked.

"I knew that you guys were the leading lady and main hero in this story. Why else do you think I'm being called now?"

"I don't understand." Landon looked to me for an explanation.

"You're the leading lady and man," Thistle spat. "That's why you haven't been called yet. I thought there was a chance I would be the last called, which would mean I'm the leading lady, but it didn't happen." She turned and glared at Aunt Tillie. "You and I are going to throw down, old lady!"

Aunt Tillie wasn't bothered. "That sounds delightful. Now, hurry up. I'm getting bored watching you guys testify. I want to get to the part where I testify."

"So get to it," Thistle shot back. "What do you expect us to say? You know everything we saw. You know how agitated we are. Why not go up there, say what you want to say, and put an end to this?"

"Now why would I want to do that?" Aunt Tillie tilted her head to the side. "That doesn't sound like nearly as much fun as causing you to suffer."

Something occurred to me and I leaned forward. I had an idea. It might not work, of course, but if it did we might be able to go through the rest of the story on fast forward. That's what we all wanted. Well, except for Aunt Tillie.

Still, if I gave her the proper opening she'd most likely take advantage of it.

"We simply want you to tell the truth, Aunt Tillie." I fought to contain my smirk when I saw the keen light enter her eyes. "I want the truth!" I yelled, gathering my courage. That was all it took to spur her to action.

"You can't handle the truth!" Aunt Tillie barked, hopping to her feet.

"And here we go." Landon smacked his hand to his forehead. "You knew exactly how to bait her."

"I did."

"That must be why you're the leading lady," Thistle groused, crossing her arms over her chest as she threw herself on the wooden bench. "I hate this world. I want to go home."

"We just have to listen to a speech first." I gestured toward Aunt Tillie. "Hit it."

Aunt Tillie ignored my sarcasm and strolled to the center of the courtroom so she'd be certain to be the center of attention.

"I'm going to tell you the truth," she announced. "I'm going to say it, and you're going to have no choice but to believe it."

"How long do you think this will take?" Landon asked, glancing at the clock on the wall.

"Who knows."

"I'm considering taking a nap."

I grinned. "That sounds like a good idea."

"Wake me when it's over." Landon leaned back and closed his eyes, something I'm sure irritated Aunt Tillie to no end. She refused to acknowledge his attitude, though. She had the floor, and there was no way she was going to cede it.

"The truth is, I'm better than all of you." Aunt Tillie added a bit of swish to her hips as she stalked back and forth in front of the wooden bench where we sat. "I'm better than you." She pointed at Sam. "I'm better than you." She pointed at Thistle. "I'm definitely better than you." She used her middle finger to point at Aunt Willa. "I am the queen of the world, ladies and gentlemen."

"Oh, this is such crap," Thistle complained loud enough to draw Aunt Tillie's attention. "Is this really what you've been building toward all night? This is what you want? You want to take the stage in front of all of us and force us to listen to your crap?"

"That's exactly what I want."

"Well, fine." Thistle threw up her hands. "Have at it. But remember, however long you make us sit here, I'm going to make you do something you hate for twice as long. I don't know what that is yet, but I'll make it my life's mission to terrorize you. That's my solemn vow."

Aunt Tillie snorted. "Yes, that was terrifying."

ALL MY WITCHES

"Let her finish her speech," Clove ordered. "She won't let us escape until she gets what she wants. I don't know about you, but all I care about is getting out of here."

"That's like letting her win, though," Thistle complained. "I don't want to let her win."

"She's already won," I pointed out. "We're at the end. She's going to get to make her speech no matter what. We have to let her do it."

"But ... ." Thistle wasn't one to give up. Conceding went against her very nature.

"We have no choice," Landon said. "Let her get whatever she wants to off her chest. The sooner she does, the sooner we'll wake up in our own beds ... er, at least the inn's beds."

"Fine." Thistle was furious, but she did as instructed. "I'm going to make you pay, old lady. Just remember that."

Aunt Tillie wasn't bothered. "Now, where was I?"

"You're better than everyone," Aunt Willa prodded.

"Thank you, Ms. Doodyhead." Aunt Tillie beamed. "So, that's right. I'm better than everyone. I'm smarter than everyone. Whenever you think you're smarter than me, you should know it's not true. It can't be true, because I'm clearly smarter than you. Heck, I'm smarter than all of you combined."

Her voice turned to a drone as I rested my head against Landon's shoulder. "I'm tired."

"Go to sleep, sweetie. It will be morning soon."

"Don't we have to listen?" My eyes felt ridiculously heavy.

"And not only am I smarter than all of you, I dress better, too," Aunt Tillie added. "I should have my own fashion line I'm such a snazzy dresser. No, really, I could totally be a fashion designer professionally."

"I think we've already heard everything we need to hear." Landon wrapped his arm around me. "Go to sleep, Bay. We're almost home."

I realized the second I closed my eyes that he was right, the tug to slip under so strong I couldn't fight it. So I didn't. I pressed my eyes shut, exhaled heavily and slid into sleep ... and thus ensured my escape.

∼

Love in the afternoon? Pfft. I would rather have a nap in the afternoon.
    – Thistle makes her disdain of soap operas obvious

TWENTY

I bolted to a sitting position in the dark, Aunt Tillie's voice still droning on and on ... and on and on and on ... in the back of my head. Something about "being young, restless, bold, beautiful and enjoying the days of our lives because we only have one life to live."

Yeah, she's not exactly subtle.

"Landon?" I reached out instinctively, hating how dry my throat was as I tried to get my bearings.

"I'm here." Landon sounded as rough as I felt.

I turned to look at him. It was dark in the room, the only light coming from the moon through the window. He rested on his back, his hand on his forehead. His shirt was off, which seemed somehow poetic given where we'd spent our night. I couldn't read the expression on his face.

"Are you okay?"

"Are you?"

"Other than the world's worst case of cotton mouth and what I'm sure will grow into a raging headache tomorrow, I'm okay."

Landon grunted as he forced himself to a sitting position. "I could use some water. I'll grab us a few bottles from the refrigerator."

"You're going downstairs?"

"I won't be gone long." He pressed a kiss to my forehead and headed for the door. I was thankful to see he was wearing boxer shorts, because in his current mental state there was a real possibility he wouldn't remember to check.

Once he disappeared into the quiet hallway, I slid my legs from beneath the covers and walked to the window. Thanks to the fresh snow – and there was a lot of it – the night seemed somehow brighter even though we were still hours from dawn.

That's where Landon found me when he returned five minutes later. He had four bottles of water and a bottle of aspirin.

"Are you okay?" He left the water and aspirin on the nightstand as he shuffled behind me, sliding his arm around my waist.

"I'm fine." I leaned against him. "So, it turns out all we had to do to escape was fall asleep."

"Now I'm betting you wish we'd stayed in bed when we first woke in that gaudy mansion."

That seemed like a lifetime ago. "Please don't remind me of that. If it had been that easy … ."

"I don't think it would've been that easy." Landon moved my hair from my shoulder so he could rest his chin there. "Are you sure you're okay? You seem … off."

"Honestly? I was looking for snow sharks."

Landon chuckled. "Anything?"

"It just looks like a mountain of snow."

Landon moved his gaze to the ground outside. "That's a lot of white stuff."

"And I'll bet it's colder than what we found when we visited that last cabin in the soap opera world."

"Probably. That only means it will be a fun day when we hike back to the guesthouse – and we're doing that right after breakfast, by the way – so we can start a fire and cuddle in front of the television the entire afternoon."

"Is that what you really want to do?"

Landon nodded. "Yup. You, me, hot chocolate and Netflix."

"I could get behind that."

Landon grinned. "Just no soap operas ... or bad science fiction movies ... or *A Few Good Men*."

"You don't have to worry about that one little bit."

THE SECOND TIME WE woke with clearer heads. We were wrapped around each other, no space between us. Somehow during the night it was as if we created one being for comfort.

Surprisingly, I didn't feel all that bad when I had a chance to wipe the crusties from my eyes and gauge my clarity and pain level.

"Are you okay?" Landon murmured. He didn't open his eyes, but he shifted so he could run his hand over my shoulder. "You're not sick, are you?"

"I'm feeling surprisingly spry. Perhaps being so active in our dreams beat back the hangover."

"Or the aspirin and water we drank in the middle of the night did that."

"Sure. If you want to be practical."

Landon's lips curved. "I feel pretty good, too." He opened his eyes and pinned me with a lazy look. "Do you want to finish what we started under the disco ball?"

"Now?" My eyebrows migrated higher on my forehead. "I thought breakfast would be the first thing on your agenda."

"I did, too. Turns out I want a little more than eggs and bacon."

"Wow. I feel so special."

"Just keep in mind, if music springs up out of nowhere and I get nothing but a montage again ... I'm going to have a complete and total meltdown."

I let loose with a loud chuckle. "I hope that doesn't happen."

"Me, too. I don't want to cry in front of you if I can help it."

"Wait ... ." I put my hand on his shoulder before he could kiss me. "Is that still the worst thing that ever happened to you?"

Landon shrugged. "It feels that way right now. I'm sure there are worse things in the world, though."

"Like?"

"Like you refusing to let me enjoy my morning and asking an endless series of questions."

"And if I stop talking?"

"I'll love you forever."

"I thought that was already a given."

"It is, but I'll totally share my bacon with you if you shut up now."

I mimed zipping my lips.

"Finally." Landon's smile threatened to swallow his entire face. "Now this is how I want to spend my day."

LANDON WAS IN A POSITIVELY chipper mood when we hit the main floor. I smelled my mother's famous blueberry pancakes from three rooms away, the heavenly scent causing my stomach to rumble in appreciation.

"I am officially starving," I announced. "I feel as if I haven't eaten in days."

"That's because we were trapped in the purgatory that is soap land for what felt like weeks." Landon slung an arm around my shoulders. "I'm back in heaven now."

I snickered. "I was just thinking that the pancakes smelled heavenly. I guess we're on the same wavelength."

"I was talking about spending time with you."

My cheeks burned as pleasure shot through me. "You don't have to lay it on so thick. I have every intention of spending the afternoon with you."

"I'm not laying it on thick. I mean it."

"Well ... thank you."

"You can thank me later. For now, let's eat those freaking pancakes. Oh, and there'd better be bacon."

We were almost to the kitchen, happiness oozing from us, when I heard a loud voice in the dining room. I recognized Thistle's dulcet tones from the foyer. She didn't sound happy.

"Don't even think about running away from me, old lady!"

Landon and I exchanged a look before pushing open the swinging door that led to the dining room. If we thought we would get out of The Overlook without running into trouble, we were sadly mistaken. Or stupid. I was leaning toward stupid.

Aunt Tillie sat in her regular chair at the end of the table. She didn't look particularly perturbed by Thistle's tone, but her expression was largely unreadable.

"What's going on?" I asked, understandably wary. "Is everything okay?"

Chief Terry sat in a center chair sipping a mug of coffee. He looked a little worse for wear, apparently his hangover raging, but the look he shot me was blasé. I felt sorry for him ... but also thankful for myself.

"Thistle just stormed into the room and attacked Tillie," Chief Terry explained. "She seems upset."

"I think she had a bad dream or something," Twila added, pressing a mug of coffee into my hand. "You don't look so bad given how much you drank last night. In fact, you look pretty together. I'm surprised."

"That makes two of us." I slid a sidelong look to Aunt Tillie and found her watching me with unveiled interest. "I also think we all shared the same bad dream."

Mom, who was walking through the door that separated the kitchen and dining room, pulled up short. She balanced the platter of pancakes and bacon she carried against her chest as she eyed me. "What do you mean by that?"

"Do you want to tell her, Aunt Tillie, or should I?"

Aunt Tillie wasn't much for threats, and she clearly wasn't worried about this potential bomb detonating. In fact, she looked eager for it to happen. "I have no idea what you're talking about," she lied.

"Oh, really, Alexis Kane?" Landon cocked an eyebrow as he sat, opting for the chair next to her so I wouldn't take it and potentially launch the family into all-out war. "I have trouble believing that."

"That's probably because you're slow," Aunt Tillie said. "Oh, and 'The Man.' That makes you naturally suspicious and often unpleasant. It's a shortcoming. I hope you overcome it eventually."

Mom set the platter on the middle of the table and heaved a sigh only a mother sick of fighting offspring could muster. Since Aunt Tillie was often like a fourth child in the family – one no one wanted to claim – that wasn't too far out of the realm of possibility.

"What did you do?"

"Yes, Bay, what did you do?" Aunt Tillie teased.

"I was talking to you, Aunt Tillie." Mom was now idling at low boil. "I can tell by Thistle, Landon and Bay's reactions that you did something obnoxious. I'm almost afraid to know what it is."

"Do you want to know what I think?" Aunt Tillie challenged.

"Not even a little."

"Well, I'm going to tell you anyway," Aunt Tillie continued. "I think that Thistle likes to talk to hear herself talk. As for these two ... they've got dirty minds. They want to eat breakfast and then head back to the guesthouse so they can do dirty things."

Landon didn't appear bothered by the claim, though I was a bit uneasy because Mom was watching me with the same look she reserved for mice that managed to sneak into the pantry.

"We're planning a day of love in the afternoon," Landon supplied, spearing two pancakes with his fork and moving them to his plate. "You know all about love in the afternoon, don't you, Aunt Tillie?"

"I'm sure I have no idea what you're talking about." Aunt Tillie's tone was icy. "If you want to turn this into a thing, perhaps we should take it into the next room. How does that sound?"

"Like absolutely nothing I want to do," Landon replied. "I don't want to talk about what happened last night ever again – at least not with you – and I want to focus on breakfast because I'm positively starving."

"All right, that did it." Mom rested her hands on the table and stared down Aunt Tillie. "What did you do?"

"Why do you assume I did anything?"

"Because I've known you my entire life."

"Yes. I believe I raised you," Aunt Tillie sniffed. "I raised you, gave of myself while thinking of only your welfare, and this is the thanks I get. My own flesh and blood is calling me a liar. It's a terrible day in the Winchester household when this happens. I'm shocked. Shocked, I tell you."

"What is with the theatrics?" Mom was utterly confused. "It's almost as if you're on a soap opera or something."

"Imagine that," I intoned. "A soap opera."

"Hey, soap operas are just like real life," Aunt Tillie said. "They're merely heightened a bit for entertainment value."

"Like say ... slapping a polar bear or getting a brain transplant, right?" Landon slid two slices of bacon onto my plate. "Or constantly being slapped across the face and ending up shirtless."

"Or ending up as a vampire by night and a judge by day," I added, smiling at Chief Terry.

"Hey, those are great stories." Aunt Tillie bit into a slice of toast. "Soap operas make the world a better place. I've always believed that."

"You also seem to believe Bay is the leading lady and I'm a supporting player," Thistle barked, clenching her hands into fists at her sides. "We're about to have a really long talk about that. In fact, you'd better get comfortable."

I looked to Landon and found him staring at me. "This breakfast isn't turning out as we planned."

"No, it's not," he agreed. "How would you feel about skipping breakfast and wading through a foot of snow to get home so I can warm you up there?"

"I'm okay with that. But, we don't have any bacon at the guesthouse."

Landon glanced at the bacon on the platter and shrugged. "I'm fine with that." He held out a hand and helped me to my feet, ignoring the way Aunt Tillie growled at Thistle.

"If you want to be the leading lady, mouth, then you have to stop acting like the sarcastic sidekick," Aunt Tillie snapped.

"You're sarcastic and still get to be the leading lady."

"That's because I'm in a category all my own."

"You definitely are," I agreed, watching as Landon detoured back to the table long enough to grab a slice of bacon before directing me toward the door.

"Where are you going?" Chief Terry asked.

"We're spending the day at home in front of the television," Landon offered. "We're watching Netflix, drinking hot chocolate and doing absolutely nothing else."

"That seems like a long walk in the snow," Mom said pragmatically. "You can stay here if you want."

"It does seem like a long walk," Landon agreed, breaking the bacon slice in half and handing me the bigger piece. "But something tells me it's going to be worth it."

"Hey, I'm not done making Aunt Tillie pay," Thistle called to our backs. "You don't want to miss what's to come."

"We're not missing anything," I said. "We're simply going to spend the day telling our own story."

"And it's going to be better than your story," Landon teased.

"Oh, just you wait," Thistle said. "My story is going to be epic – and so is your punishment, old lady. You'd better start running now!"

We left them to their fight. It wouldn't end. We knew that. It was a soap opera, after all. The story there – much like Thistle and Aunt Tillie's fight – was never meant to end.

It wasn't such a bad thing – once you discounted the polar bear, of course.